"Nightmarish and powerfully unnerving, ˌ៲ᴀᴄ ᴠ……᠁

labyrinthine and profoundly complex portrait of queer relationships, obsession, routine, and destruction. Wilde's prose is masterfully controlled even when so much of this devastating story feels like a kind of demented stream of consciousness written at the end of the world. One of the most disorienting and upsetting works of queer fiction I've encountered this year."

—Eric LaRocca, author of *Things Have Gotten Worse Since We Last Spoke*

"*I Can Fix Her* is one of the saddest yet most beautiful fucking things I've ever read. Wilde demonstrates a mastery of experimental narrative structures and my god... the prose! Phenomenal."

—Paula D. Ashe, author of *We Are Here to Hurt Each Other*

"In this ferocious tale, strata of bitterness, jealousy, and dashed expectations form an unstable foundation for Johnny, who desperately seeks a reconnection with her aloof, enigmatic ex. Wilde's incandescent prose blazes, but don't let the beautiful, poetic imagery of *I Can Fix Her* fool you—this story digs into the psychological bedrock of why we hope that the people we love will change to be exactly what we need and crave, even when deep down we know the truth."

—Lindz McLeod, author of *Sunbathers* and
The Unlikely Pursuit of Mary Bennet

"*I Can Fix Her* seamlessly blends the surreal and the horrific to capture a relationship so awful it breaks time. Compulsively readable and vivid as fuck, Rae Wilde's prose is as fierce as it is hot, hot, HOT. Do not miss this toxic bonbon of a novella!"

—Wendy N. Wagner, author of *Girl in the Creek* and *The Deer King*

"A relentless, obsessive spiral through time, *I Can Fix Her* thrusts you into a cosmic fever dream of queer desire and destruction. With prose as haunting as it is visceral, Wilde unravels the terrifying lengths one will go to preserve love on the brink of collapse. Dark, gripping, and unforgettable, this book refuses to let you go—even as it pulls you into its unrelenting depths."

—Mallory Pearson, author of *Voice Like a Hyacinth* and *We Ate the Dark*

I CAN
FIX HER

RAE WILDE

HORROR

HORROR

Copyright © 2025 by Rae Wilde
Cover by Matthew Revert
Interior illustration by Brett Mitchell Kent
ISBN: 9781960988515 (paperback)

CLASH Books
Troy, NY
clashbooks.com
Distributed by Consortium
All rights reserved.

First Edition 2025
Printed in the USA.

CW: Stalking, murder, gore, domestic violence, emotional manipulation, blasphemy, graphic sexual content.

This is the last one, you son of a bitch.

TABLE OF CONTENTS

MONDAY

This is the part I have to watch. When Johnny spots Alice, head thrown back in laughter at the Speakeasy Café, with a vague sense that she's been here before. The rest will be educated guesses based on layers of memory. **Trust me, the details do not matter.**

Johnny's unnerved by something altogether too familiar about those pale waves tumbling down Alice's shoulders, the angled quirk of her smile, her untamable aloofness. And the woman beside Alice leans a bit too close, dark curly hair brushing Alice's platinum. She's giggling at what Johnny assumes to be her own joke as they share an oversized, fruity-looking drink through two straws the color of Pepto-Bismol. The drink is teal. Fuzzy shapes of red and green sink to the bottom of the glass. Likely gummy fish. Likely old gummy fish gone hard with time.

Inside Johnny is a yawning gap; a gap that aches at the sight of her once-lover, bathing some other woman in attention that once was Johnny's, once belonged, wholly, to her. And yet, inside the aching, yawning pit of abandoned promises and daydreams gone stale, is the foul lingering of a sour love. Love like the sweet burn of sugary rum.

Johnny *has* been here before. She's stood in this spot, surrounded by white patio tables, matching chairs with checkerboard cushions. Below strung twinkle lights and within spitting distance of 4th Street. Where the buildings are brick, close, and uneven, clamoring onto one another like the street is a mouth of crowded, leaning teeth.

Johnny should turn and leave. Her hips tilt with a shift of her weight, as if she's preparing to do just that; but she can't leave. A memory holds her there with a force much stronger than logic.

She's chosen one from six months ago. Another one at the Speakeasy Café, when Alice and Johnny, strangers to lovers, became strangers again. The café was very much the same. It was night, though, during an unforgivingly cold winter and beneath an unusually clear sky. Johnny had looked up at the stars. She could see so few through the light pollution and layers of smog, and yet she knew they were there, spattered like freckles across the face of an endless expanse. She'd thought of incendiary gasses, illuminating distant planets, even after the void had swallowed them. They were generous, she'd thought. It had reminded her of Alice.

"I'm going to Berlin," Alice had said. Johnny was back on earth, and Alice's pale eyes were glittering, hair swept back in a braid so intricate, Johnny couldn't figure out how her fingers weaved the pattern. Silverware clinked on plates, and a stray cat brushed against Johnny's leggings.

There had been too many beats of silence. The question of *how long* went unasked, and the invitation to join Alice went unsaid. Johnny's hands folded in her lap. "So, that's it?" She'd nudged the cat away, its fur leaving a slick of moisture on her calf, enough to invite the evening's chill.

Alice's fork had twirled inside a loop of zucchini noodles, tines whining on ceramic. "Don't make this a *thing*."

Johnny'd thought to beg, to offer to pay for her own ticket. Hell, she'd thought to offer to pay for Alice's ticket. But recalled a time further back, when Alice, carrying the leftovers of a filet, had ignored a whining dog in the street, even though the vertebrae jutted up through its fur like its very bones were reaching out for help. She'd recalled how Alice had carried the takeout box all the way home, just to drop it in the trash. She'd recalled how Alice detested desperate things. So, Johnny did not beg. But she still paid the check.

And now, in an echo of then, Johnny glances to her right, to the table where it happened. Where she'd sat, dumbfounded, bill in hand, fumbling for her wallet. Where Alice hadn't argued with her or reached for her credit card. Not really.

Johnny just stands there, like a flea-bitten stray. She looks from Alice to the other woman, that curly-haired, too-femme-for-Alice woman, and back again. Johnny knows the singularity of Alice's stare. It once focused on her.

It's not real, she wants to yell to the curly-haired woman. But that would be crazy. That would make Johnny the *problem*, just like Alice always almost said. Just like Johnny always feared.

Johnny breathes out the words she wanted to yell. She doesn't see me when she turns, doesn't remember that I'm standing here, but I see the stumble in her movement, the inertia of her foot, how it scrapes the sidewalk instead of lifting cleanly off the ground. I'd reach for her, would wrap my fingers around her elbow to guide her away, if I could.

Alice's little black dog is already bounding over. I'd stop it, everything inside me screams *stop it*, but Lucy the English Bulldog sinks her teeth into Johnny's ankle.

Alice calls out to the little rogue beast.

Johnny freezes in her tracks, feeling the eyes of a lost-love on her back. She worries Alice will think she is following her. She only stumbled across a picture Alice posted. Not really *following* her. Just curious. Curiosity is reasonable after six months of silence. Now, rubber soles smack sidewalk, Alice is coming for the dog, and it all begins again.

No internet in Berlin? No phones?

The familiar argument plays again in Johnny's head, but she doesn't even get to the good part before Lucy is pawing at her pant leg, whining. She's forced to scoop up the English Bulldog to keep her from darting after a passing elderly man. He yelps, startled as Lucy growls in Johnny's arms, snapping his direction. The man sidesteps, and his wrinkled face finds new places to fold with his displeasure.

Johnny thinks people like Alice shouldn't own dogs. That dogs should be with people who can love you back.

Lucy wriggles in her hold. Her potbelly is fat and warm and pink and bald. She gnaws at Johnny's thumb knuckle. Alice must've bought her this godawful, bedazzled collar. It's no wonder she bites.

"Johnny?"

Alice is closing the distance between them, just six feet away now. If Johnny turns around, she'll know it's true. I understand why she just stands there a second. She's thinking, *Maybe if I don't acknowledge time, it won't pass. I'll just stand here, Lucy slung across my arms, Alice remaining six feet away.* But a maroon SUV passes, a gaggle of kids screaming or laughing in the backseat. Rubber soles bounce louder off sidewalk. Time is passing nonetheless.

"Didn't know you were back," Johnny says. A lie.

Her eyes focus on Alice's feet first. Converses. Beat up. Grungy. Johnny thinks she's wearing them ironically.

Probably some sort of test, where if she were to say, *Oh, I love those Converses*, Alice would snicker-laugh, that ambiguous sound, indiscernible from mockery.

Johnny sets Lucy down near the Converses.

Her eyes trail up Alice's slim legs. Freshly shaven. A little nick of jealousy cuts like Lucy's serpentine teeth. Was she planning to fuck curly-hair? Is she still?

Johnny tells herself she doesn't care.

Ripped, cutoff denim shorts frame the place Johnny's head has rested a hundred times. Not rested. Flourished upon. Nestled inside. Worked over 'til Alice screamed to God. A white cotton crop-top reveals Alice's navel. She's too old for that. *You're too old for crop tops,* Johnny wants to tell her. *That's a Gen Z thing.* But she doesn't.

"I got back last week."

Johnny meets her eyes. Clear as glass. Icy pools. She thinks she could dive in. Thinks she could happily freeze. Or drown. "Great."

"Hey." Alice's chin dips, she scratches the base of her skull behind her ear, light refracting off of her gold stud earrings. "I'm glad we ran into each other." She glances over her shoulder at curly-hair, whose stare has narrowed, then turns those glacial eyes back on Johnny.

"Yeah, I was just heading…" Down the street is a laundromat, Johnny knows that wouldn't make sense. Alice knows Johnny has a washer/dryer.

"I was leaving too," Alice says. "One sec."

Fastening Lucy's matching leash to that hideous collar, Alice hands the leash to Johnny and scurries back to the bar. After summoning the bartender to bring the check, she exchanges a few words with the curly-haired woman, who, in turn, scowls in Johnny's direction.

Johnny's waiting on Alice again. She wonders how this happened, Lucy happily panting at one end of the leash, her anxiously waiting at the other. The curly-haired woman's scowl melts away when Alice kisses her cheek, and Johnny thinks of returning the dog and making an excuse to leave. But it's only an exercise in thought. Something Johnny believes she *should* do. Because who would entertain the whims of a person like Alice? A person who could just buy a ticket to Berlin? A person who might've doted on Johnny for a time, but not as an equal. Loved her like she might love a little dog.

Johnny doesn't come up with an excuse to leave. She's a moon now, stuck in Alice's gravity. All those imagined arguments that played out so clearly while Johnny took scalding showers, the ones that ended with Alice realizing how wrong she'd been, ended with tears and apologies. Those arguments static-out like white noise. Johnny is trapped in orbit.

The bartender approaches the pair at the bar with a printed check. Alice pulls a wallet from her back pocket, but the curly-haired woman shoos it away. They exchange furtive smiles before Alice returns her attention to Johnny.

For the briefest moment, Johnny's distracted by Lucy's tugging at the leash, another attempt to nip a passerby.

Alice's focus lands squarely where I stand. She takes deliberate steps toward me, toward Johnny, toward us.

"**Don't do this**," I say. But if Alice can hear me, she ignores it. If she can see me, she pretends she doesn't. Alice links her arm through Johnny's, and they set off in the direction of Alice's new apartment, a building appropriately named *The Encore*.

Over the short walk, Johnny and Alice exchange a number of phrases, most of them pleasant, none of them worth repeating. The only words of note come when the women stand at *The Encore's* outer door. It has an iron frame. Bars meet at neat angles, too thinly spaced for a body to slip between. Johnny lingers on the step second from lowest. Alice's key ring is looped around her fingers when she says the only important thing.

"I want to explain."

Words like a barbed hook, keys like a reel.

And Johnny follows Alice through the iron door with its orderly lines, through the ordinary wooden one, and down a hallway pocked with flyers. An HOA meeting. An estate sale. A lost cat. The elevator buttons are yellowed with wear, linoleum floor peeling up at the edges. Lucy grabs hold of a curling corner, exposing a new sliver of subfloor beneath.

Johnny ignores her buzzing phone, and when the elevator opens with a ding, Alice says, "Home sweet home," an octave too chipper for the dreary hallway.

Brass numbers hang crooked on apartment 607. With its red paint flaking, it seems lonely at the end of the hall. If Alice has neighbors, they must be out, or quiet, or dead but undiscovered, for not a sound penetrates what must be thin walls, not a single sign of life.

"It's private," Alice says, fiddling with her key ring. Johnny catches that the first key Alice tries doesn't turn the lock, even when Alice tries to shield it with her hand after the fact. She wonders whether that's the curly-haired woman's key, nestled between Alice's and the little bronze one for the mailbox.

The door opens and inside is dingy grout, off-white tile surrounding it, formica countertops a murky shade of green, cabinets old and crumbling. This is Alice's home. Through the long cut of a narrow hallway, Johnny spies a slice of the living room where a second-hand couch is draped with a long, leopard print blanket undoubtedly hiding a stain. In spots where the sun-faded floral wallpaper has peeled back, a hairline crack stretches taut across the white of the drywall.

"Nice place," Johnny says, feeling a twinge of satisfaction at knowing the woman who broke her heart is living in a real shithole.

Either Alice doesn't notice the sarcasm, or she ignores it. She's too keen not to notice, so perhaps she really does want a clean slate, to wipe away the animosity and begin again. "Can I get you anything?" she asks.

Or Johnny has been staring too long, and Alice is shifting the conversation through feigned politeness. "No, thank you." Johnny knows it's time to look elsewhere. She angles her body, glances outside, mimicking someone who is just another visitor, an old friend, someone laissez-faire. The view through the window is industrial, corners of buildings visible if Johnny cranes her neck to see.

Alice tosses her keys on the countertop, the clatter sending Lucy skittering in the opposite direction, dragging her leash. She sits lightly on the couch, tapping the jaguar blanket where it covers the cushion beside her. "Will you sit a minute?"

Johnny takes a detour around the coffee table, unclipping Lucy's leash and resting it atop her crate. She tucks her bag behind the crate before sitting where Alice indicated. Her back is too straight, knees too stiff. She can't remember how she used to sit around Alice. If she could, she'd mimic that. But she can't remember. So, Johnny sits rigid and awkward, all right angles like the iron door.

Alice's fingertips graze the shaved side of Johnny's head, a tickle that travels down Johnny's neck and settles deep in her chest. "Your hair is short, like I like it."

The compliment is a warm wash that tugs Johnny's mouth into the shape of a smile, but it dies as quickly as it formed.

"Are you still at City College?" Alice asks, tucking her hands in her lap.

"No." Johnny leans back into the cushions, a facsimile of cool even as her features stiffen. "It didn't work out."

"They fired you?"

"Wasn't a good fit."

Alice shrugs. "No big loss. I didn't like the way that professor ogled your ass."

"He did not," Johnny says, picturing Alice watching Professor Culligan watching her, seething with jealousy as the professor sneaks a peek. A tiny smirk dimples her cheek before she forces it away.

"He did," Alice insists. "I wish you would get out of academia. It's a rhetorical circle jerk with no real-life application. You should do something with your hands. Remember when you DIY'd that bookshelf? You dragged that pallet six blocks."

Johnny relaxes, thinking how she struggled with the unwieldy thing up three flights of stairs, how Alice noticed.

"Well, I don't know what the training is like, but I was thinking, you'd make a great carpenter."

"Just now you were thinking that?"

"I think about you a lot," Alice says. "I thought about you while I was in Berlin."

"I thought about you too." Johnny's mind replays voicemails. The calls, straight to machine, didn't leave breadcrumbs. But the voicemails Alice must've received. *Why didn't you call?* Johnny thinks to ask. She doesn't ask, because she's lovestruck, not dumb. Johnny knows the answer: Alice didn't want to call. *Why did you go to Berlin in the first place?* That one's a little better, but still off. Johnny's asked that before, at the Speakeasy, at the white patio table, a stray cat circling under a sky full of careless stars. Johnny wants to ask, *Do you love me?* But she'd never get a straight answer. Johnny's phone buzzes in her pocket.

"You need to get that?" Alice asks.

Johnny checks the phone, clicks to ignore the unsaved number, then tucks it away.

"Something important?"

"No." Johnny leans back onto the sofa, folding arms across her chest.

"You seem different," Alice says.

Johnny wonders whether it's *different good* or *different bad* or *different enough to interest Alice*. "It's been a while."

"Not that long."

"Six months," Johnny says. The longest crawl of days and weeks in her life.

Alice reaches for a coaster on the coffee table, adjusts its position to align with the table's corner. "People can change in six months."

"Can they?"

"I think they can."

Alice takes her time with the words, like she's savoring the taste of them. "I think I've changed."

It's a subtle thing, the way Alice's thigh inches closer to Johnny's. The heat of her bare flesh travels through Johnny's denim, a tiny press that says, *I'm close. I'm here.*

"You're angry with me," Alice says, smoky in a way that sounds like, *Come to bed with me.* She swipes something off the rim of Johnny's glasses, a gesture disarmingly familiar, like a dance they've done a thousand times, a waltz only the two of them know.

Johnny is angry. She can't remember a time she wasn't angry with Alice. But the anger seems an isolated movement among the many steps of their dance together. Infatuation, need, and that bitter, sour love come along with the anger, taking beats in time.

"I'm sorry I left." Alice's fingers spider crawl over Johnny's thigh. She is taking the lead position. Johnny is tempted, feeling the rush of being twirled away, spun headlong into the waltz and humming a desperate, minor key. She steadies herself, placing her hand on the empty cushion beside her, diverting her focus to things that don't dance, won't sweep her away. Things like facts and science and logic.

"I'm sorry I left *you*," Alice says, leaning closer, her stomach remaining flat even with the curve of her body.

Back, back, back up. Running fingertips over the pilled fabric of the couch. Away from the swirl. Johnny will not be sucked down. She fixates instead on Alice's thinness. Wonders whether it's a matter of science: genetics and metabolization, an inherited preference for lower fat foods. What's the ratio of genetic code to socialization when it comes to the formulation of preference? As long as Johnny wonders, she won't allow herself to feel.

There's math to consider. A formula inclusive of the distance between Alice's home relative to nearby nutritional sources and the variety of foods offered therein. Not as simple as that, there's also the variable factor of digital access, the linkage of apps to more distant options. But those receive a negative impact component proportional to increased cost. Delivery fees. Extraneous tips.

I'm sorry I left you.

That's not even considering the denominator of exercise, whether deliberate or coincidental. Commutes by foot or bicycle. Even walks to trains and buses and the short trek to catch an Uber can add up, calorically speaking. But Johnny leans toward a psychological cause. That Alice believes the space she's allotted ends at the limit of her bones (aside from her breasts and ass, which society makes allowances for, provided they can be seen—not too seen, mind you—and enjoyed by the general public).

"It's okay," Johnny says, calmer now.

"I needed some space."

Johnny wants to tell Alice she's already created so much space around herself, she didn't need to cross an ocean to make more of it. But she just says, "I know."

"Stay for dinner." It's not a question, nor a demand. It's a statement of fact and a foregone conclusion. "The Chinese place you like delivers here."

Johnny nods. Alice dials and orders. She doesn't need to ask any questions, and rather than feeling insulted by the presumption, Johnny's comforted by the order's familiar rhythm. "Crab Rangoons, a pint of wonton…" Alice speaks into the receiver.

Johnny checks her own phone, telling herself she is interested in the missed calls and is not just passing time until Alice's attention is back on her. Her voicemail has been full for months, so she does not check it. Mostly thirty-second snippets of static. Telemarketers. Autodialers, where the system isn't prompted by the beep, so the robot just hangs on the line.

The text messages, she sees.

Today 5:38pm

Potential spam: Call me 0-112-358-1321

Potential spam: Seriously

Potential spam: Johnny, call me.

Potential spam: JOHNNY

Johnny has no patience for distractions. She thinks I'm nobody, nothing, unimportant, and she blocks my number.

She has forgotten me and doesn't want to be interrupted when Alice offers to show her pictures of the Berlin trip. She wants to look carefully, at the background and foreground. Each time Alice flips to the next, Johnny braces for an auburn-haired German woman with an easy grin of sexual satisfaction, or a Spanish tourist partially obscured by hotel-white sheets. If she sees that, maybe Johnny will do what she planned to do. But that never happens on Monday, and the photos are of the usual stuff: oversized beer glasses brimming with foam and amber ale, graffiti under a bridge with a moody filter, clouds through an airplane window. Off-center snaps of blooming flowers.

I wish I had been with you, Johnny thinks. *I could've photographed you beside that graffiti. The peonies would've brought out your eyes. It would've been better if we were together. I wouldn't have ended up hating you.* But she doesn't say it.

Alice parrots a few German phrases she learned in her travels. Her accent is bad. Johnny doesn't have to know anything about German to know her accent is bad. Three knocks land on the front door, and Alice hops up to answer it saying, "Must be our food."

Johnny tries to commit the hard, German sounds to memory. The exact shapes of their square edges. She'd like to look them up later. She'd like to see if any of them translate to, *I love you, Johnny. I love you and I always have, even if I don't know how to show it. All I ever want is you.* But the sounds get jumbled. Mixed up with the pleasantries Alice exchanges with the delivery man, and Johnny forgets them.

"I'll grab plates."

Balancing the paper bag between elbow and hip, carrying a spoon and a fork and soda cans, Alice returns and sets the coffee table. Johnny tears open the bag, placing the paper menus aside and divvying up the meals: soup for Alice, Rangoons for herself. She grips a deep-fried triangle, grease leaking onto her thumb and forefinger. "Who watched Lucy while you were gone?"

Alice takes her time opening the soup lid. She presses up on the lip, freeing it one inch at a time as steam vents through the widening hole. "My mom. I dropped her in Connecticut before I flew out."

Alice's mother is a selfish, waspy woman, preoccupied with country club gossip and courting a third (or was it fourth?) husband. They've never gotten along. Either Alice was eager enough to leave to face her rich-enough-for-Coach-but-not-Hermes mother, or she is lying and Lucy stayed with someone else.

Johnny eyes Lucy in her spot on the floor, as if close inspection might tell her whether Alice is being truthful.

But Lucy doesn't say anything, she just chews a rawhide strip she dragged from under the couch.

Alice stirs the soup, churning noodles from the bottom to the surface. "I heard Brittany is pregnant."

"Her and the baseball guy?"

"Mark, yeah."

"I thought they broke up," Johnny says.

"Back together."

Johnny rolls her eyes. "And is she happy about it?" She can't imagine being happy about heartburn and stretch marks and volumes of discharge.

Alice swallows a spoonful of soup. "She's pretending to be. I think she just likes fantasizing about a different life than the one she has."

Johnny crunches down on a Rangoon's crispy edge. "People always think kids will solve their problems. As if taking care of some other dependent creature will unlock a portal to a world where all their problems melt away and they get a clean slate."

"Do you think it's possible?" Alice asks. She lets the question hang there, fishing out a slice of carrot and examining it on her spoon. "For people to start fresh?"

A waltz drums in the back of Johnny's mind, a cadence of one-two-three, so she thinks about molecules instead. The invisible bonds between them in that slice of carrot, ionic and covalent, the only things keeping carrot from soup, soup from spoon, spoon from Alice's hand. She thinks about the bonds between herself and Alice, how they twist and widen and shrink to form the shape of a story. "Maybe," Johnny says. *One-two-three.* "But not by making a kid."

I know, but Johnny doesn't know, **that they can't start fresh**. But they can begin again. In fact, they must.

One-two-three.

One-two-three.

Johnny forgets to blow steam off her Rangoon. She takes a bite.

When the soup is tepid and Johnny's stomach can't stretch the width of another single drop of greasy cream cheese, Alice clears the remnants of dinner. She dumps broth and flat soda down the drain and stows the garbage in a trashcan tucked in a cabinet tucked beneath the sink.

"I guess I should go," Johnny says, standing in the kitchen's entryway.

Alice pumps two squirts of lavender soap into her palm and runs the faucet. Johnny lingers. "Is that what you want to do?" she asks above the sound of rushing water.

Johnny says nothing. She doesn't want to go.

Alice tears a length of paper towel from the nearby rack, dries her hands, and chucks it into the trash before kicking the cabinet closed. She leans back against the countertop, slanting her pelvis out and toward. Johnny thinks how easy it would be to unbutton her shorts and slide them off. "Do you want to stay?"

Johnny says nothing. *One-two-three.*

Alice slinks past Johnny to the bedroom and Johnny follows, watches her pluck the crop top over her head, undo the button on her denim shorts. Alice tugs Johnny's pants down to her ankles, making it easy for Johnny to step out of them.

Johnny stays.

She grabs Alice's hips, pressing her mouth to their hollows. Her lover arches into her, skin tasting faintly of salt; and when Johnny's hand slides between Alice's legs, she is greeted by a slick swell of desire. With a sharp breath, Alice yanks Johnny up, entering her in turn. With the fullness of Alice inside her, Johnny closes her eyes and exists in a universe filled to its limit by just them two. Through a tangle of sheets, Johnny feels a body beneath her that curves and has bones placed in ways familiar. A body that clenches and shudders following movements Johnny's practiced. *I could do this forever,* she thinks, as Alice writhes to a climax. *I want nothing else but this.* Her lover cries out: ragged gasps and pleas to God and Johnny's name on her lips. *God may love you*, Johnny is tempted to say, *but not better than me.*

They lie together, facing popcorn ceiling, Johnny studying the pattern of water stains. There is no rat-a-tat-tat of blossoming emotional fireworks, just artificial, orange street light battering its way through the curtain from the city outside.

"That was amazing," Alice says, voice husky with shallow breath. "You were amazing."

Johnny laces an arm over Alice's waist and pulls her in close. Their bodies fit together, barely a seam between them. "I missed you," Johnny whispers. "I'm sorry if I scared you away."

Alice wraps her arms around Johnny's arms wrapped around her. Moments of silence pass, swollen with anxiety about what might have been, anticipation of what might still be. "Let's try again," Alice says. "We can be better this time. Change where we need to. For each other."

This was all she wanted, all those lonely nights. Nearly driven mad by the simple denial of having Alice nestled in her arms. "I can change," Johnny mumbles into the space behind Alice's ear.

"You've always been so special," Alice says, then extricates herself from Johnny's winding limbs and goes to the bathroom to brush her teeth.

For a moment, Johnny is nearly happy. She can change. She knows she can. She would do anything for Alice, change anything, and the worst parts of her recede when her lover is near. But across a mountain range of pillows, Alice's phone glows on the nightstand. Face down, its blue light reaches between the screen and the faux wood of the nightstand's top. Light that signals information. A message catapulted through space, intended for Alice and Alice only. And yet, it's just there. Words beaming into molded plastic, wasted on carved grain and imitated swirls that can't appreciate them.

Johnny considers reaching for it, stealing those words for herself, discovering whether Alice has ensnared that woman from the Speakeasy Café; but Alice is already spitting, palming water and rinsing. So, Johnny doesn't check the phone. She crosses the room and extends her hand, and Alice places the still-warm toothbrush in her palm, smiling. Johnny tops the bristles with wintergreen toothpaste, pretending not to notice the buzz of Alice's phone behind her.

In the mirror's reflection, Alice's eyes dart to the sound, then dart back. She says, "You are so, so special to me."

And Johnny believes she can change herself, but more importantly, change Alice. It doesn't matter whether that curly-haired woman is sending texts. Johnny is the one here with Alice. Johnny is the one sharing her toothbrush, her bed. The only one who can fix her.

TUESDAY

Imagine Johnny, waking. Hair mussed, short, brown spikes pressed in odd directions, pillowcase creases in her cheeks. Hazy remembrances of sleep scamper away, and Johnny blinks the blur from her vision, finding beside her a dream made flesh.

Alice sits up, as if stirred by the movement. Reaching, back arched, hands to the sky. Johnny counts the vertebrae along her spine. She doesn't know how many vertebrae a person should have, but she counts twenty. That should be the right amount, she thinks, unless exceptional people have more vertebrae, in which case maybe most people have about fifteen, and Alice has more than average. She counts one more time as Alice makes a pleasant cooing sound, arms falling to her side. But when her counting reaches the base of Alice's neck, Johnny notices.

"Your hair," she says.

"It's a mess, I'm sure." Alice twists with a coy pout, taking Johnny's cheeks in both hands and planting a tight-lipped morning kiss on her mouth. She draws Johnny up to a sitting position beside her, plucking a fallen eyelash with pinched fingers. "Make a wish."

Johnny closes her eyes. Makes a wish she dares not even think too loudly. *I wish it could be like this forever.* She blows, directing the puff of breath away from her lover. Eyelash gone, Johnny runs a curved finger over the blunt edges of Alice's haircut. "It's short."

Alice palms the blunt ends of her bob, squishing them into her jawline. "Do you like it?"

Johnny thinks back to the night before, long platinum strands draped over Alice's pebbled nipples. Long strands. Some stuck to her lip. She had to brush them away. "I do, it's just, last night—"

"You don't like it?" Alice's amusement cools to suspicion.

Johnny gets anxious. "It's not that."

"I needed a change," Alice says, casting the blanket off her legs and turning away to dismount the bed. "I think it suits me."

"But when did you…?" Johnny struggles against lingering fatigue, grasping for any recollection of chopping sounds in the night. She squints through still-bleary eyes to look for snipped hair in the attached bathroom. The grout is dingy, tile still a putrid shade of beige. But no hair lies on the floor.

The faucet gushes.

Toothbrush. Toothpaste. Alice works up a foam across her front teeth. Molars. Top. Bottom. Spit. "I dunno, not long ago."

"I just—"

"We're starting fresh," Alice says. More water: Gargle, rinse, spit. Alice turns with a hawkish stare. "Don't be weird. I'm gonna walk Lucy."

Johnny watches short-haired Alice tug an oversized sweatshirt over her head and shimmy on a pair of cotton shorts. She doesn't want to argue, so she's consumed with watching. Watching, watching. So swallowed by it, she pads across the room to watch Alice get Lucy from her crate and—

Lucy?

In Lucy's place is not Lucy at all, but a bulldog. A bulldog, bulldog. Must be nearly 100 pounds of black bulldog, roughly the shape of Lucy but increased in size. Not an overpriced, shrunken version you might find peddled at a beachside strip mall, bred into miniature, into snorting gasps from a smashed snout. No.

"Lucy, come," Alice calls the dog, unphased. Seemingly unaware that French bulldog Lucy is now a thundering, knotty beast.

Johnny's frozen in the doorway. All her careful, measured articulation from the night before collapses to an infantile vomit of words. "Everything's different," she blurts out. "Your hair is short and Lucy…she's fucking huge!"

There's a long moment of quiet. Long enough for Johnny to question her sanity, her vision, her sobriety, her memory from the night before. In that long, empty moment, Alice grows only more stern.

"Things change," Alice says, a wrinkle forming between her eyes. "I thought we talked about that."

If you could see Johnny, you would see her calculating canine growth but failing, because it's not her expertise. You'd watch her consider the contents of the bathroom waste bin, but being unable to see inside from her position on the bed, not knowing if there's shorn blonde hair in there or—

"We talked about *us* changing. To be better. Better for each other not…"

Alice huffs with an incredulous shake of the head, the edges of her bob catching on her ears. "You believe in change or you don't, Johnny." With that, she clips new-Lucy's collar to the matching leash and is out the front door in eight heavy steps.

Johnny goes swirling. She's stuck in a *one-two-three* and she got out of bed too soon and she didn't drape the covers over her shoulders and scroll social media like she usually does; so she's cold and confused, a shiver wracking her shoulders.

This is not a new feeling, in fact, it's too familiar, this deep-seated dizziness. She needs something firm, something to grasp, something rooted to the earth and not to mercurial Alice.

Johnny steps into the living room. She looks to the couch, for the leopard print blanket, but it's gone. Maybe Lucy ate it, some chemical in the fibers responsible for the unnatural growth, she wonders. But in the same beat of wondering, she knows that doesn't make sense, the blanket being inedible and lacking nutritional value, and feeling quite sure that if blankets held some power of exponential growth, scientists would have discovered that by now and somehow exploited the trick for profit. Were that the case, blankets would cost thousands if not tens of thousands, controlled by pharmaceutical companies and distributed frugally, and only through a bureaucratic system of managed payers who would ensure deductibles were met and medical necessity was in place and the like. Johnny had slept with a blanket just the night before, so she felt sure none of the former was the case.

Does Johnny believe in change?

She's still cold, so she returns to the bedroom, crawling back under the covers and drawing them over her goosed shoulders, up to her neck. Alice's phone charger snakes across the empty nightstand. She's taken her phone. Must've snatched it quickly, a fluid motion Johnny missed.

Johnny misses things sometimes. Especially around Alice.

She decides there are bigger things in flux than length of hair and size of dog. She doesn't want to feel so tossed about, so seasick, so churned by a force much greater than herself, but Johnny can't admit that. Instead she tells herself she cannot miss the point this time, the big deal: the second chance. Another opportunity to make it work with the woman she loves.

That word. *Love.* It falls short in her mind. She wants to think of a bigger word. A longer word, perhaps. One meatier, with weight. She thinks back to the rectangular, German sounds Alice made the day before, the details too faded to mimic. German has nice, hefty words. Johnny thinks they must have one that could be sufficient to hold her feelings for Alice. She makes a mental note to learn some German. Surely a weighty German word for love would hold her down, ground her to the earth.

Johnny always thinks this on Tuesday, and on Tuesday Alice's hair is always too short and Lucy is always too big. And Johnny has already blocked my number. And from where she lies on the bed, the wall is hiding the view of the billboard where I'm standing. Standing and unfurling a vinyl sign. **She won't see me**, not now and not later, but she will see the sign.

I'm getting ahead of things.

So what if Lucy stretched and Alice's hair shrunk? Johnny figures if she can change and Alice can change, the relationship between the two will change. She is not a fool, has not been tricked, and, most importantly, is not a fool who has been tricked *again*. If the relationship changes, the end result changes, id est, Johnny loves Alice and Alice loves Johnny and Alice doesn't leave. She scrambles out of bed, determined to make herself look like someone Alice would want to change for, someone Alice would want to love. Johnny crosses the room to the bathroom and squeezes a strip of wintergreen toothpaste onto Alice's toothbrush.

Faucet runs.

In a scenario where Alice and Johnny and the relationship and its likely end are all changing, other things can shift too.

Brush foams.

It follows that they would, considering their environment is shifting around them.

Spit.

Johnny decides the only important things are those bonds between herself and Alice and shaping them into a proper story with a proper ending. One in which Alice doesn't leave.

Rinse.

Johnny's hair has always been short. That much is the same. Brown tresses kiss her brow bone when pushed forward, shaved sides that tickle Alice's palm when she runs her hand across the prickled hair. That's good. That's what Alice likes, maybe even loves.

Her eyes are also brown. Less good. Unremarkable. Forgettable, even. If she leans in and inspects them closely, they've got little gold flecks, which is nice, but nothing like Alice's powder blue. Peering into Alice's eyes is like looking through a window on a frosted winter day. Or a porthole to a churning ocean swell.

Johnny thinks hers are like looking at a leather couch with brass studs.

There are no clothes in Johnny's bag. Just the other things. Things she doesn't think she'll need now, but she does need her black cutoff and the new jeans with the holes in the knees. The shirt fits her just right, accentuating her modest biceps and drawing attention away from her chest. The jeans are new, which means Alice hasn't seen them before, which means maybe she'll like how they slouch at the waist and let a little hip bone peek out, and maybe she'll think some other woman suggested them—better even, bought them for her. Maybe she'll get jealous and possessive and all but drown Johnny in attention.

Johnny has a plan.

She grabs her phone, battery indicator red at 4%. The time is 8:16. She'll be late for work. Johnny taps out a quick message to her supervising professor, explaining that she's ill and won't be in. She could run home, grab the cutoff and the jeans and a charger and come back. But if she leaves, she'll need a reason to come back. Her options are: leave and make herself more like someone Alice would love, but risk the possibility that Alice would not invite her back for another chance, or stay and remain brown-on-brown-Johnny.

Johnny slumps down on Alice's bedside.

The swinging of a door. The creak of neglected hinges. The chitter of paws on tile. Alice finds Johnny, her cheeks flushed pink from the walk, ribs expanding and contracting.

"You're stuck in that head again, aren't you?" She draws her thumb from Johnny's temple to chin, and Johnny's sucked into those glacial eyes, icy and deep enough to sink the unsinkable. "Come with me."

Johnny accepts Alice's hand, follows her out of the bedroom and past the crawling crack in the living room drywall. Lucy ducks into her crate and curls up with a plush toy. Alice motions at the sofa, and when Johnny sits, curls into her lap.

"Wonder if…" Alice starts, tucking an arm behind Johnny's back. *Wonder if* is an old game. A silly one Johnny made up when they were new, still mixed up in that sublime glow of endless possibility. "Wonder if you won the lottery."

It's a strong start. Alice is dreaming up their future. "I'd take you to Scotland."

"You'd buy me a castle?" Alice smirks and traces a swirl through prickles of Johnny's hair.

Johnny recites Alice's dream, somewhere far enough from here to feel like another time altogether. "I'd buy you a castle by the sea so you could watch waves break from your window."

"You'd dig me a moat?"

"I'd dig you a moat and fill it with crocodiles."

"I don't think Scotland has crocs."

"I'd ship them in."

"To keep people out?"

To keep you in, Johnny thinks. She plants a kiss where Alice's neck meets her shoulder. "Only the ones we don't like." Johnny raises the stakes. "Wonder if we had a daughter." *Oh.* Saying it aloud clutches at Johnny's heart. A daughter would bind them together. For so many years. For forever. Alice might recoil from the notion, and Johnny wishes at once she could pluck the words from the air before Alice hears them.

"I'd braid her hair," her platinum-blonde-bobbed lover says. "I'd teach her archery."

Tears prick at the corners of Johnny's eyes. She wants to say, *That's all I want, a life and a daughter with you.* But that's too much, so she says, "Why archery?"

Alice mimes pulling a bow from a quiver, lining up a shot with one eye closed. "It's badass," she says, drawing back the imagined bowstring. "With flair." Alice lets the invisible arrow fly. The wall opposite cracks, a hole the size of an arrowhead punched in the drywall.

Johnny's eyes are fixed on the new pock in the wallpaper. Having accepted that perhaps people change, and with them, everything else, she considers a new theory. "Wonder if we could wonder our way to real."

That one sits a minute, while air pools around them and grows stagnant. The AC kicks on. What if her love was big enough? To break reason. Physics. Logic. Johnny grows hopeful at the thought, then frustrated at the hope of the thought. She remembers she's angry with Alice. Remembers long nights and empty mornings. "Wonder if you hadn't left," Johnny says.

Alice's lips draw tight. "I'm not leaving now." She pushes off Johnny's lap, sitting cross-legged in the spot next to her. "Wonder if you grabbed me some water." A mischievous grin and Johnny gets up, crossing the living room to the kitchen.

"Ice?"

"Yes, please."

Johnny fishes a handful of cubes from the icebox, then realizes she doesn't know where Alice keeps her glasses. She checks cabinet to cabinet, frigid water dripping through her fingers and rolling to her elbow. With each failed attempt to find the glasses, the ice continues to melt, her palm aching. All that love she feels for Alice, and she doesn't even know where she keeps her glasses. It's the last cabinet she tries, and by then, the tips of her fingers are numb. When glass and water and ice have been properly sorted, she returns to the living room.

"What is this?" Alice asks. Her forehead is crinkled into a scowl, and her eyes are fixed on Johnny's dying phone.

A gut drop. Johnny grips the glass so tight she thinks it might shatter.

All the warmth and hope and future dreaming from just moments before distills into chilly dispassion. "Brenda Ramburg?" Alice coughs out a humorless laugh. "You've been stalking me."

She knows. Johnny thinks about hours and days. Weeks and months spent in infinite scroll. She knows about the masked follows and likes and requests for digital friendship. The searching. "It's not what it looks like." A clumsy cliche, and Johnny sets the glass down on the coffee table to hide the tremble in her wrist.

"That's not even a real name. You could've at least chosen a real name for your fake accounts." The trail of water from Johnny's wrist to her elbow sends a chill through her body.

"I just…"

Alice is still scrolling, taking in data, knowing and learning more.

"I just wanted to—"

"You're *obsessed.*" The word is a hiss. "It's not healthy." Alice shakes her head. "It's not normal."

"I just wanted to see if you changed!" The echo of a rage restrained bounces off the walls and floor, which at once feel too naked, too bare.

"This is too much," Alice says, tossing Johnny's phone on the couch cushion beside her.

"Don't do this."

"This is why I went to Germany."

Johnny rounds the coffee table.

"I had to get away."

She gets to her knees in front of Alice.

"We're not good for each other."

"I'll delete them," Johnny says, taking Alice's hands in hers. "It was terrible, it was crazy of me, but I just missed you!" She pulls Alice's fists toward her chest, tugging her body closer. Within Johnny's chest, an organ pumps blood, fast and hard and desperate. She would hand it over to Alice, slimy and thumping. She thinks she already has. "Don't you know what it's like to miss someone? I love you."

Alice draws back, worry and sadness in the lines of her face.

"Please, let me show you how much."

"What if we can't change, Johnny? What if this is just who we are together? Jealous. Broken. Dangerous."

Alice's hands go limp in Johnny's, but Johnny squeezes. She would never let go, never release this grip. She would offer up her twitching heart to receive Alice's in return.

"What if we can't be together," Alice asks, "no matter how hard we try? What if we're not supposed to be?"

"You don't believe that," Johnny says, sealing off the place inside her that dares to consider it might be true. "I'll change. *We* will change. Think how good it could be, if we just get it right."

"It's a pattern," says Alice. "You and me, hurting each other."

Johnny weaves herself tighter into Alice's thighs. She tangles their bodies together as if her arms and Alice's legs are all the pieces of them she wants to save. "Don't give up on me," she says. *I have never given up on you.*

Fingertips comb Johnny's hair. She shuts her eyes, embracing the tingle of nails against her scalp. "*Johnny*," Alice says like a sigh.

Can't we just try? Johnny thinks, warm tears beading her lashes and rolling through fine blonde hairs on Alice's thigh. She smears them away. "Can't we just try?"

Alice nods, tracing the lobe of Johnny's ear.

The afternoon is a stiff display of Johnny changing. She deletes Brenda's accounts, showing her phone so Alice can see. Apologies pile up in stacks until Alice insists they not talk about it anymore, and turns on a rerun of some show with a laugh track that plays when jokes aren't funny and fills the frigid silence between them with a chorus of pre-recorded joy.

When night falls, Johnny asks, "Can I stay?" and Alice offers up an old t-shirt and loose fitting sweatpants and an acquiescent nod of the head.

They hold one another in the quiet.

Alice ignores the buzzing from her phone on the nightstand. Johnny grips tighter to Alice, pressing one ear against the pillow and muffling the other against the side of her lover's head. She tries not to hear, but the buzz-buzz-buzz invades her private, in-between place of sleep and awake. It must be that woman from the Speakeasy. Or a woman from Germany. Maybe both.

Johnny thinks of the contents of her bag, then pushes that away and pulls Alice closer. This is her big chance, and everything is changing now. Johnny has to change too, has to trust that they can change together. She tells herself to dream of love.

She dreams instead of the wild, of predators and prey, the metallic scent of blood.

WEDNESDAY

On Wednesday, it snows.

Johnny needs to bury the evening before. The ugliest moments, the blue light flash of Johnny's phone on Alice's face, the loitering void of almost losing her, dims and dies under the cleansing white of fresh winter. Johnny needs to keep Alice, preserve the possibility of the two of them. She prunes pieces of time toward her purpose. She smothers the world in a pristine blanket of snow. She is an expert on forgetting.

Johnny and Alice peek through the bedroom window as crystalline flakes drift down from a powder sky. Snow drifts pile up, one-two-three stories, and the billboard across the street wears a frosty beard. The slogan reads: *Call now!*

There's a phone number too. Tucked beneath the powder where Johnny cannot see.

"It's good you stayed over again," Alice says, rubbing her crossed arms as she clutches herself. "Your place must be totally snowed in. I'll turn on the heat."

Johnny checks her phone. Dead. "Did you get anything?" she asks. "A severe weather warning?" Alice's bare feet clap against the living room tile. There's a click as she adjusts the dial. "Yesterday was what? In the 80s, I think."

"Something like that," says Alice. The heat kicks on, burning off dust and pumping the acrid scent through the vents.

"I've never seen anything like this." Johnny is still looking out the window when Alice returns to the room.

"Climate change." Alice shrugs.

Johnny's imagining people beneath that blanket of snow, covered up like ants in a dirt hill. Is snow heavier than dirt? Flesh is softer than an ant's carapace, more tender and malleable. "Do you think they're okay?"

"Who?"

"The people lower down."

"Which people?"

"Lower down."

Alice tugs on a flannel shirt and fluffy boots. "Let's make the best of this. I'll light a fire."

Johnny follows her to the living room where a stone fireplace dominates the main wall. Cut logs are stacked in a leaning tower inside, and Johnny is sure there was no fireplace yesterday or the day before. But then, they hadn't needed one. Monday and Tuesday had been warm. The snow came and the need for heat arose and the fireplace appeared to meet the need.

When Alice claps her hands, Lucy, black as midnight with three serpentine heads, her body sleek and scaled, spits fire across the center of the room. The wave of heat sends Johnny backward, flames roaring, wood cracking under the sudden blast. The mouth of the hearth stretches up to the ceiling, yawning eight feet wide. Lucy, the creature that answers to Lucy, narrows three sets of yellow eyes in a satisfied grin. Her long necks weave and braid together, dipping and bending like kelp in a deep sea. In a shiny blur, she turns and kicks off, smashing through the sliding glass door, launching from the railing, and sprouting leathery wings at the apex of her leap, just in time to glide off into the white-out sky.

"Warmer now?" Alice asks, rubbing her palms together.

Glass falls in sheets from the borehole in the patio door. Ice crystals form along the jagged perimeter, and Johnny's breath hangs thick in the frosty air. "No," she says.

"Come closer." Alice wraps an arm around Johnny's waist, pulling her toward the inferno nestled in the wall. "Reminds me of Christmas." Flames dance in her irises. "Remember that Christmas?"

Christmas with Alice is something Johnny remembers. It happened last year. They wore matching Santa hats. Burnt sugar cookies. Wore PJs all day. Johnny had a record made of Alice's favorite songs. Alice gave her a teal teddy bear, un-wrapped, with the price tag still dangling from its ear. Johnny glances around the living room, through the buckled radiance of fire where no fire should be. "Where's your record player?"

"Oh." Alice hugs her body tight. "Probably in storage."

Where is the record I got you? is what Johnny means to ask.

"You still have Teddy." It's a conclusion, not a question. "What did you name it again? Cleo?"

"Clea," Johnny says.

"Clea," Alice says. "Clea, Clea, Clea. I'll remember now." Her phone buzzes in the bedroom. She follows the sound and Johnny is alone with the fire and then, "Do you mind if Brynne stops by?"

"Who?"

"Brynne." Johnny doesn't know the name, although Alice says it like she should. "Just for a few," Alice says.

Johnny roils, dizzy and sick. There is so much she will accept: short hair, a fireplace, a dog-turned-dragon. But this shouldn't be happening. It needs to be just them two, nobody else because—

A knock at the door.

"That's her!" Alice chirps, sweeping from the room to answer.

Through the front door comes the curly-haired woman from the Speakeasy Café, bundled in a scarf and overcoat, the perfect amount of powdery snow speckled in her hair.

"Brynne, Johnny. Johnny, Brynne." Alice helps the woman out of her coat, hanging it on the hook behind the door. "Will you stay for dinner?"

Johnny doesn't understand. They just woke up and now—

"Johnny is cooking. She's been planning quite the feast," Alice says.

"I'd love to stay," Brynne answers. "Vegan?"

"Always."

Johnny looks from one to the other, then past the fire and through the shattered glass door, where the sun bows low in the sky. Everything is moving faster now, changing faster. Wooly clouds are trimmed in bronze beams. *The sun is a star*, Johnny thinks. She forgets that sometimes, but the sun is a star. Not *the* star. Just a star. Only *the* star for those on Earth, who see it brighter than everything else.

In the terminus of the horizon, a dark shape dives. Just a speck. An arrowhead that might be a tear in a dream or a dragon or a French bulldog called Lucy.

Inside the apartment, drywall crumbles around yesterday's pockmark.

Within the pockmark is a chasm, within the chasm is a void, and within that void, shimmering liquid black. An iridescent, beating darkness. A living darkness. Red numbers on the oven clock read 6:36. "Any allergies?" Johnny asks, though she's not sure why. It feels rehearsed, like she's following a script she long ago memorized, though she can't recall its purpose.

Johnny forgets things.

But I remember.

"Nuts," the woman says.

Johnny nods, walking into the kitchen like a moon caught in orbit. Pans lay on unlit burners, cooking oil sits beside the stove. "Do you have any…" Johnny trails off. She's not vegan. She doesn't know how to cook vegan food.

"Seitan?" Alice asks.

"I love seitan," Brynne says.

"Fried, right, Johnny?"

"Fried," Johnny says, though she doesn't know how to fry seitan. Johnny doesn't know what seitan is. She doesn't know how to fry anything.

"Where's Lucy?" Brynne asks, Alice leading her to the living room.

The couch is gone, replaced by the roaring fire which is smaller now, just fireplace-sized. The women squeeze together in an overstuffed leather loveseat with brass studs. New. Not the secondhand couch that was here before. Alice and Brynne needed a loveseat and so a loveseat appeared to meet the need. They face away from Johnny and the kitchen, looking out over the winter-crowned city. Around their shoulders is the jaguar blanket. Real fur. Head on, snarl bared beneath green glass eyes, and jaws resting in the crook of Brynne's neck.

"Lucy's exploring," Alice says, indicating the hole in the sliding glass door. "You know her. She'll be back by morning." Does she say it to Johnny or Brynne? Why would Brynne know Lucy?

Johnny finds a package in the fridge labeled *seitan* and pulls it from the shelf. Oil pops in the pan, though she doesn't recall turning on the burner, or pouring the oil. "How did you get here?" Johnny asks.

Silence from the living room.

She adds, "I just mean, the weather. The snow."

"Oh," Brynne says. Johnny can't see her face, but she imagines Brynne's eyes rolling. "I'm from Ithaca. We're used to this kind of weather. I wore my coat."

77

"But the roads…" Johnny starts.

"Were cold," Brynne finishes.

In every version of this, Brynne and Alice exchange a mocking look. Johnny doesn't see it, but she feels it happening, a tightening in the air like a hand around her throat. Like fingers squeezing, closing her airway, she can almost feel the blood vessels pop in her eyes. Red numbers scroll across the oven clock: *0-112-358-1321*, pouring endlessly like a hemorrhage. She thinks of predators and prey. She smells blood.

Smoke slithers off boiling oil, unfurling in dread-leaden ribbons. They buck and billow, soaking into her hair and eyes and nostrils, wild as a dream. Johnny feeds it seitan, which the oil gobbles up with a hiss.

"Ready?" Alice asks.

Through the kitchen keyhole cutout, a table stretches the length of the living room. Candelabras burn gold beneath candlelight. Long white tapers dribble wax to a linen table-runner that's black and red and mustard yellow and patterned. China gleams in ornate setups. Metallic lips on ladles. Smaller plates stacked atop larger ones. Serving spoons. Tongs. Napkins folded into flowers and real flowers, hydrangeas, overflow a silver basin centerpiece, dragonflies flitting from one blossom to another.

Alice sits at the head of the table. A gilded chair frames her head, and beyond that, melt drips from the borehole in the sliding glass door. Brynne, at her right hand, wears a ballgown. Blue satin. Or silk. Johnny doesn't know which because Johnny's not an expert on fabrics or fashion. They're talking about, laughing about, *that Chinese spot in Harlem.* The lady with the Maltese. Or was it a poodle? They can't remember, and the Lyft driver's accent. Russian, they think, but it might have been Bulgarian. Brynne imitates the back-of-throat position of his words, and Alice chuckles, trying her own hand at *hyelloh!* A memory shared between just the pair. A *one-two* hiphop Johnny doesn't know.

Fireplace, gone.

Loveseat, gone.

Outside, snow changes shape. Collapses.

When Johnny looks down, she's dressed in a three-piece suit with tails, seated opposite Alice at the table's far end. Twelve feet of oak stretch between them, adorned with heaping plates of broccoli, Brussel sprouts, candied carrots, fried seitan, leafy salads with cut strawberries, fluffy rolls, and all manner of lidded sauce boats wreathed in steam.

"A feast," Brynne says, a fork in one hand, knife in the other.

Dinner is played in grating keys of silver gnashing porcelain. Brynne and Alice scrape salad onto plates with a nightmarish fervor, speckling the runner with shades of wilted green. Alice stabs food and lifts it, but never eating, never eating while Brynne chews, chews, crunches, chews. Ice clinks in glasses, metal on metal on wood on china, *clink clink*, a clash of a symphony of hunger of need of giggles

Johnny can't join—a song of the damned like a choir of demons screaming hoarsely screaming and all of it, the sound, the smell of boiled broccoli, the—the cackling at the man with the mustache on the subway and the party that wasn't a party at all, and the sum of it, all the sounds and sights and smells of it taken together makes Johnny nauseous; the changing and the laughing and the wrongness and nothing is as it was and the hacking. The hacking cough and the strained, weak whisper of strangled breath and Johnny thinks for a moment she has panicked, has had an attack, but then Brynne stands with such force the chair shoots out behind her, legs shrieking against the tile. Hands enclose her own throat, amber eyes bulge and the vein pops in her temple.

Brynne's iris bleeds yellow. It's dissolving, staining the whites around it, and the coughing stops, and Brynne's chin juts up and out. And silence. Stagnant, desperate silence.

"She's choking!" Johnny cries.

Alice blots the corner of her mouth with a cloth napkin.

Brynne gapes around air that doesn't pass her straining lips.

Johnny stands, freezes, the table shuddering under her force, bottles clinking. Bottles clinking that catch her attention. Emerald glass, the label reading *Peanut Oil*, a skull and crossbones drawn beneath. Is that what she used in the kitchen? Is that how she fried the seitan?

Brynne's fingernails rake her purpling neck, leaving white then yellow then pink railroad tracks. The allergy, Johnny remembers, but had she used peanut oil… That she didn't recall, but she does recall that she forgets things. She often forgets inconvenient things and Brynne's eyes are rolling and the grip on her neck goes slack as she slumps, mid-air, folded for the longest fraction of a second in time, then collapses, head smacking the corner of the table on the way down.

Alice looks. Goblet in hand and red wine leaking down her chin.

Blood pours. A hemorrhage. Soaks curly hair. Following the channels in the grout. Pumping. Spreading. Until it pumps and spreads no more.

By Thursday morning, the apartment is thick with a metallic scent, and Brynne is dead.

THURSDAY

Every Thursday, Brynne is dead. Whether by knife or rope or the single iteration in which Johnny surprised her in the bathroom and she slipped and cracked her head on the porcelain sink. Johnny can't recall those loops, but **I hold them for us both.**

In this version, tears gather in the corners of Johnny's eyes, loosening the last clumps of Monday's mascara as she gazes down at the lifeless body.

"Why did you do it?" Alice asks, staring down at the corpse. Dim light from a hesitant sunrise filters through her platinum hair and falls meekly onto Brynne's death-blanched cheek. Brynne's eyes, cast open, bulge in her broken skull, fixed and unseeing. Johnny follows her phantom line of sight to a spot on the wall where the fissure that became an arrow pock has stretched to a chasm. Inside the chasm, that iridescent void of nothing.

"I didn't mean to hurt her," Johnny says. "I didn't know."

Alice crouches beside the corpse, brushing a crusty strand of curly hair off Brynne's forehead. "She told you about her nut allergy. I heard her."

"I don't remember using—"

"You were jealous." It's a sharp shift, Alice's eyes from Brynne to Johnny. "You thought there was something between Brynne and I, and you couldn't stand it."

"I did not think there was—"

"Hah!" Alice cries, rising to her feet. "Liar."

"And so what if you were seeing each other?" Johnny tries. "I would never have…"

"Of course you would," Alice says, advancing. "You've always been jealous. Possessive. That's your problem." Her stiff fingers jab into Johnny's shoulder.

I just love you, Johnny thinks, wanting all the fire in Alice. *I need you. There's always someone or something between us. Why can't you need me in the same way?* Dappled light casts clustered shadows upon Alice's neck and shoulders. Not dappled light, Johnny realizes, but pinkish spots.

"It's ugly, Johnny."

"I already told you," she says, "The oil was in the pan…" *Hives? Are those hives spreading across Alice's shoulders?* "It was an accident. I never would've—"

Alice digs her fingernails into the sides of her skull, making an exasperated sound, then paces a back-and-forth line. Behind her, a gentle shushing. The sound of water moving. Beyond the sliding glass door, a wave moves across the city street, carrying at its crest a shelf of ice. Alice's pink marks darken to brown semi-circles, the surrounding skin yellowing like Johnny's only ever seen in jaundiced newborns.

"This is why I had to go!" Alice's black eyeliner drops down the inner corners of her eyes, on either side of the bridge of her nose. Her smile is one of bitter knowing, of having a worse fear confirmed. It's joyless, predatory, and her pointed canines lengthen, reaching over her bottom lip.

Outside, water spills between the bars of the patio's railing, flooding the porch. "Alice…" Johnny says, gaze locked on the rising water.

"You wonder why I had to fly 4,000 miles. Well, here's why!" The spots darken to black, becoming more defined. "You think you love me, but you don't. You want to own me. Control me. Love is not possession."

"Alice."

"You're obsessed with me, Johnny. *Obsessed*." This time the word is more growl than hiss. A foot of water swirls in alternating currents, lapping against the glass. "It's sick, really. You're sick. You know that, don't you?"

"Alice!" Johnny screams it, pointing at the snow melt. The water advances impossibly fast, climbing the sliding door. Tops of waves splash through the borehole left by

Lucy, and a patio chair is yanked into the current, hurled onto the flooded city street.

"Shit," Alice says. "Lucy!" She crouches and calls through the opening, face pressed to shattered glass. "Lucy!"

She bellows against the yellow skyline. A rogue wave crests, rears up, pushes forward, gaining speed as it courses between buildings, through alleyways of steel. Windows fold like spun sugar in its wake; the billboard is consumed and swept under, and above the place it disappeared, at the tsunami's bent neck, dark shapes break the roiling surface.

"Lucy!"

Tentacles flick and flail, water froths around the protrusions which wind in every direction, circling, dipping, and popping up again, kicking up spray as the behemoth rushes ever closer.

Alice steps away from the glass. "She always comes home."

The ground vibrates. Walls rattle and the air hums a low note as the wall of seawater and melted snow stretches up and up and farther upward until it's reached beyond view, until it spans all the height of nature's gargantuan aspect.

Johnny braces for the impact, eyes locked on the shifting, fragmented shadow obscured by filthy blue. She has never felt so weak or small, so meaningless in the face of destructive power that is not hers. Power that does not care for her. Does not *care*. The wave is a wall, a monstrous wall, and within its bounds swims a creature beyond definition. A tear forms in the corner of Johnny's eye. For the first time, she understands fragility. She comprehends the meaning of *unstoppable*.

Johnny is reduced to trembling atoms. Bones seem to chatter and clink together. Her blood is kinetic, nerves sparking with disabling electricity, her muscles useless, rigid, for all the microscopic scurry within. The sky, the earth, and all mankind's tinkering is washed in utter black as the tsunami reaches high enough to snatch the sun.

It hits.

Johnny's on her back. The force reduces the present to pain and a slippery brush. She does not hear sound. *Sound* implies a foundation of quiet on which to build. A flat basis upon which something stands in opposition and can be perceived as a singular, identifiable thing, an isolated entity with beginning, peak, and end, with definable edges and phonic qualities—an up, a down, a key, a rhythm: minor or major, harmonious or grating, a word or a feeling or a string of them. There is no *sound*, for nothing, nothing is left to Johnny but the ravenous, cosmic roar. Even the notion of existing without the deafening, carnivorous yowl is flattened to dust the instant the bellow is born.

The wail, the bawl, the yawp, the progeny of snow and wave and sun is the last sensory experience of what Johnny understands to be an ending. *The* ending. She loses control of her faculties, a coward rendered blind by the hulking figure of a screaming, unfeeling death. In the space of a blinking fraction, a thought slips through Johnny's neurons and hits a synapse: *We are going to die.*

But Johnny is wrong.

The thought hangs there. It isn't cut short. And Johnny realizes she's squeezed her eyelids shut. When she opens them, just a squint, she makes out the furling and unfurling spindles of Thursday's Lucy, appendages too great in number, too fragmented in configuration to make sense of, before the creature slides into a widening gap in the drywall.

Alice presses her body against the sliding glass door, the space where Lucy bore a hole the day before. Those ten-by-eight-foot panels of glass are a porthole, the eye through which Johnny sees the underwater churn of a choppy sea. As if the city were an ocean, as if the apartment were a submersible, Johnny peers through the glass and into dark water, where a school of tuna dip and dart. Their silvery, flashing scales catch what little light they can, and the tuna move, the school bending and breathing into shapes as if thinking with a central mind. For a singular moment, the fish take odd positions. They seem to form a number, 0-112-358-1321.

In a beat, they're gone. The cosmic roar is replaced by a sandy quiet. Particles shush and rain gently onto rocks unseen. Bubbles, far-off, cascade and trickle and pop. A rocking, a tide, slants right then left in a cradling rhythm. Kelp spirals through the blue, caught in a deep current.

The weight of the water, the pressure of the sea flooding the streets of New York should obliterate the glass. They *should*. Alice's body could not possibly create a watertight seal, even pressed there as it is, and even if it did, the slight woman should never be strong enough or gain enough leverage to hold her position against the might of a million liquid tons of force.

And yet, all is not as it should be. And yet, Alice stands there, holding back an ocean.

Johnny beholds something impossible, the bending of logic and the flexibility of physics. That Alice Leigh has never been obedient, is something Johnny knows. Not obedient to social nicety and not obedient to laws, neither human nor universal. What I would tell Johnny, if I could—What I would scream into her ringing ears **if I could bridge the gap between us**, is not something I came up with on my own. It's something we heard. From someone else—Maya Angelou. **I would say**, *Believe her, Johnny. Believe her as she shows you who she is.*

Past the waifish figure of Alice, still pressed to the glass, a massive figure drifts through what once was a passage between buildings. It swims between the shattered windows of what had been the sixth-floor apartments, but is now no more than fodder for manmade reefs. A gray whale. It croons a melancholy song. Fins fanning in a slow-motion flip.

Johnny lies there. Looking. Two things are true at once, both incomprehensible, both plain as day: A whale moves through 10th Avenue; and Alice Leigh is immovable, in every sense of the word.

Alice asks for duct tape.

She's still angry, and when Johnny grabs some from her bag and hands it over, her eyes are slitted with a feline glow. "This is your fault," she says, tearing a strip with too-long, too-sharp teeth. Her back seals the hole, then she rolls, hooping her weight through her hips, and fastens strip by strip until the ocean is restrained by rippling slats of silver. Alice throws the roll of tape at Johnny, who catches it against her chest. "Brynne is dead."

Brynne is dead. Johnny had almost forgotten about Brynne, but the corpse is sprawled on the floor between her feet and Alice's, half her twisted body on the now seawater-soaked area rug.

"I think you should go," Alice says, the last word rolling through a growl.

Johnny glances at the ocean outside. "Go? How?"

"Just go."

The apartment is soggy with the scent of brine. A kelp strand sticks to Johnny's calf. She glances at the door. Imagine Johnny, thinking of grabbing that brass knob, of walking out. Facing the unknown. Willing to drown. And she is willing to drown. But not without Alice.

"No," Johnny says. "It wasn't my fault she died, and I'm not going."

"You're not going," Alice says. "You're not going," she says again, having never acquired a taste for the flavor of defiance. Her back rolls into a hunch, head dropping between her shoulders. Golden eyes stare into Johnny's as Alice says, "I should've left you at the café. It was a mistake to try again."

It was a mistake to try again. Laughter rolls from a deep, twisting place in Johnny's chest. Once the first peal escapes, there's no stopping it. The sound spirals out like an eruption, bringing with it a prickle at the back of Johnny's nose and a stream of tears too long pushed down. "It's *you,*

Alice!" she cries. "The problem is *you.* Why can't you love me in the way I love you? If you didn't dangle yourself in front of Brynne, if you didn't fly the fuck away when you felt me getting too close, I would have nothing to be jealous of. But you torture me! Torment me."

"Get out!" Alice says. Her nails lengthen, curling into claws.

Johnny, still laughing, tears dripping off her chin, squares her shoulders with Alice's. Now that the truth has started pouring out of her, she can't stop it. "No. You want me sometimes, but never enough. Because you're fucked up! You don't love me? Sure. But only because you don't love yourself."

"Get out!" The words sink into a low register as the human shape of Alice distorts into a new form. Fur grows from every area of exposed skin, her clothing is torn off with the resizing of limbs, and when the transformation is complete, Johnny faces down Alice the jaguar, Alice the jungle cat.

Johnny thinks of the door. The cat's tongue dips out between her jaws and flicks the air as the animal pants. Her rounded ears pin back, weight shifting toward her rear as if preparing to pounce. She would rather be *something* to Alice than her stranger. Even if all she can be is her prey. "I'm not gonna fucking go."

The big cat, Alice, makes a soundless leap. Meaty, taloned paws connect with Johnny's chest, knocking her easily to the tile floor. The smell of the wild, sweat and dirt and blood and fresh kills overwhelm her. There's barely a moment of pain as the jaguar's teeth glide through Johnny's neck, just a strong tugging sensation as it tears out her trachea.

The cat pants, its body weight undulating with the pattern of breath. With the pattern of Johnny's beating heart.

Johnny bleeds.

Her vision narrows to two, blurry porthole windows. Staring back at her are slitted, feline eyes. Warmth soaks Johnny's hair, crawling up the back of her skull and oozing down the nape of her spine. Her fingertips numb. Then her hands, then her arms, then her torso. Jaguar Alice flexes whiskers. Her ears round and come to the top of her head. Johnny's never studied big cats, knows almost nothing about them, but she swears it's a look of pity. Maybe even a look of remorse. A sandpaper tongue rakes across Johnny's cheek. Then again. It feels affectionate. Contrite.

I'm sorry, Johnny thinks to say, but her throat is in the belly of the beast, and even if her vocal cords were intact, Johnny dies before she can mouth the words.

FRIDAY

Death denies Johnny on Friday.

The chemical scent of house paint wakes her. It's dark, all sense of time stripped from the third-floor apartment. She does not remember dreaming, and her thoughts come in piecemeal fragments. The sliding glass door is painted streaky black, drying in clumps. Whether night or day, Johnny is no longer sorry. Her hair sticks to the tile where the blood has dried, weaker strands are ripped out as she sits.

"You killed me," Johnny says, reaching for her throat. It's crusty but intact.

Alice pokes her head out from the bedroom, once again a woman. In her hand, a paintbrush drips globs. "I only beat you to the punch."

There's a pounding in Johnny's skull. She's slow to stand. "No." The room feels as if it might tip over. She braces on the hallway wall, letting her vision spin. "No. What do you mean?"

"You know what I mean." Alice sets the paint can on the floor. The scent is thick, almost unbearable, and it burns Johnny's eyes. "I went through your bag."

The room steadies and Alice grabs a bag from beside Lucy's crate. She drops it on the table, letting the contents clatter inside. With the same two fingers that just Monday were inside of Johnny, coaxing her to climax, Alice fishes a knife from the bag, then lays it on the coffee table. She pulls out the length of black rope, setting it beside the knife, then the roll of silver duct tape. Alice arranges them next to one another, lining them up, one-two-three. "When you had that duct tape yesterday, I got to thinking," Alice says, adjusting the slant of the knife to a perfect ninety degrees. "I knew you were pissed, but this seems overboard, don't you think?"

Johnny's mind gets busy: She knows. She knows about Brenda Ramburg and the stalking and now the tape and knife and rope. Alice will leave her. Alice will certainly, absolutely leave. She will flee from the apartment shrieking like a banshee. *My ex is crazy! She's trying to kill me! My ex is crazy! Please help!* But when Alice looks up at her, there's no fear on her face, just curiosity, both childlike and sinister.

Alice lifts the duct tape, digs a fingernail under the lip and frees a length with a ripping sound. She bites and tears, pulling off a strip about four inches long. "Is this what you wanted?" It's a playful challenge born of complete exhaustion. Alice holds each end so the strip is parallel to her mouth.

Johnny doesn't know what to say. Her mind is empty of excuses.

"You want to kill me, Johnny?"

This is how it ends, she thinks. Lucy's frozen in her crate, whites showing around her black, beady eyes.

"Is that why you stalked me to the Speakeasy? To kill me?" Alice tilts the strip of duct tape back and forth.

Stalked. "I wasn't going to—" The sound of denial is all wrong. It's meek. Unsatisfying. False. She wants to grip the truth with both hands, cleave to it, dig in her fingernails.

Alice flips the tape back and forth, letting it stick to different fingers like a juvenile game. Alice thinks everything is a game. Thinks Johnny is a game. A joke. Something to be toyed with.

"You want to kill me? I'll make it easy for you. Look!" She points to a glob of paint on the glass. "I even blacked out the windows." Alice sticks the tape to her face, holding the flap over her lips. "I would rather be dead than stuck here with you." She smooths it across her mouth, then sits on the sofa and joins her wrists together, offering them up to Johnny and eying the rope.

The quality rope. Black thread, strong, smooth. Even when planning revenge, Johnny couldn't imagine skimping on frayed, prickly rope. It's light in Johnny's hand as she unwinds the loop and drapes the center over Alice's wrists. Glacial eyes watch every movement, unafraid.

Does she really think that Johnny won't do it? After all she's done to hurt her?

She loops the rope over Alice's wrists once, before realizing it's all wrong, more coy than violent. Alice doesn't love her. Not then and not now. And how dare she? *How dare she?*

She pushes Alice face down onto the sofa, yanking her arms behind her and tying her wrists tight with unforgiving knots. Alice doesn't flail, doesn't cry out. The only sound she makes is an uncomfortable keen when Johnny jerks her arms up at a severe angle and grabs Alice's phone from the coffee table.

"Passcode," she says.

It's hard to hear the shape of words through the tape, but with enough repetitions, the phone unlocks. Johnny opens the photo album, scrolling down to the hidden folder.

Face ID required.

Johnny holds the phone to Alice's face. Her lover's features are pinched with discomfort.

Face ID failed.

Face ID failed.

Face ID failed.

A quick rip of the tape, a flash of the screen, and the folder unlocks. Johnny secures the tape back over Alice's mouth, surprised when Alice doesn't scream. *Does she really want to die?* Johnny wonders as she scrolls. *Or does she think I'm too cowardly to do it?*

The folder is a treasure trove of lingerie mirror selfies and elicit shower pics obscured by steam. Some, Johnny recognizes. Others, she doesn't. The most recent show a woman, strawberry blonde with square-rimmed glasses, front teeth a bit too large for her features, cheek pressed to Alice's and toasting with a beer bug Johnny recognizes from the Berlin trip.

"There was a woman in Berlin," Johnny says. And then again. "There was a woman in Berlin." She knew, Johnny assumed it must be true, but to see it, to have it confirmed, hurts. It fucking hurts. "How many more are there, Alice?" She opens the text messages, finding Brynne right at the top. A quick scroll up reveals emojis: kissy face, wet, hot.

I love the taste of your pussy.

Come get it.

Nobody makes me scream like you do.

I'll drop off Lucy in the morning. Thx for watching her!

"How many?!" Johnny screams, tossing the phone so it flops onto the sea-soaked area rug below. Lies. All of it was lies.

She pushes Alice's shirt up, exposing her scapula, the vertebrae between. Fine hairs rise along the length of her spine. Johnny snatches the knife from the table and drags it, smoothing those hairs back down, keenly attuned to the soft scraping sound it makes against Alice's flesh. The blade is thick, curved at the end with a mean-looking hole. A hunting knife. Johnny bought it a month ago for a different game. A hunt. She bought it to hunt Alice.

When Johnny traces the perimeter of the lowest rib, Alice pushes her head into the sofa cushion to muffle a pained groan. A red line raises, a bloody little half-moon. Would Alice still dampen her cries if Johnny slid the blade between those ribs? She thinks not. She thinks that scream would buck against the duct tape, that Alice's head would wrench back, tears pouring from her eyes, smearing the remnants of yesterday's makeup.

How is Alice so slight beneath her? More puzzling, how does she manage her smallness while still occupying all the space in Johnny's life? Ribs expand and contract. Johnny's flat palm on Alice's exposed back feels the pounding of her lover's heart. Perhaps Alice *is* afraid, blood drawn, wrists bound, mouth sealed. Perhaps the weight balanced on her back feels less familiar, more capable of violence.

But for all the drama in the pumping of blood, Alice lays still, unsquirming, even as Johnny lets the knife's tip rest at the base of her skull. "You left." Johnny says.

Alice raises her head enough to nod, enough to expose the welling tears in the corner of her right eye, then presses her head back into the cushion. Johnny drags the blade so it pulls up a layer of skin down the spine, but not deep enough to cut. "You left and I wanted to kill you."

Alice makes a garbled response, and Johnny needs to hear, so she reaches around and rips the tape from Alice's lips. For a moment, Johnny's breathing stops. She thinks Alice will scream. That she's made a mistake. But Alice just says, "I know," the words thick and clotted.

Johnny studies the knife. A knife is a versatile bit of ingenuity. She thinks, *A knife is like a woman.* Both have the power to provide sustenance, nurture a life, both have the power to take life away. *My woman is a knife.* The blade pecks Alice on the nape of the neck, deepening to a French kiss that slides between vertebrae like parted lips. Alice's cry starts high, then drops in register, then grounds out in a gurgling, bubbly choke.

That salacious, wily knife slips through Alice and lodges itself in the couch fibers. Becoming part of the woman it is so much like. Skewered together, stitched, two become one. Alice shutters. Twitches. Then lies still.

Finally, Johnny is alone.

There's a rustle from the hole in the wall where the creature Lucy crawled inside. Alice's blood seeps into the puddles of seawater, staining them wine dark. The apartment, destroyed, feels alien around her.

Johnny is terribly alone.

The hem of Alice's white shirt frames the drawn paws of a jungle cat. Johnny glances at the skin beneath the thin fabric, finding a jaguar tattoo over Alice's shoulder blades. Johnny's arms wrap tight around her lover's limp body. "Don't leave me."

From the wall comes a rumbling. The hole in the wall, the hole that started with hope, with wondering their way to real, has grown cavernous, wide and tall enough for Johnny to step through. The void stretches, swirls of indigo interspersed with the blackness.

An inky stretch of space seems to reach from the wall, curling across the room like a finger of smoke. Darkness snakes over the coffee table, joining with Alice's spilled blood where it streams from the couch, twisting into a cane of candy red and indigo black. The cane splits into spaghetti rivulets, which worm their way into Alice's nostrils and parted lips.

On Friday, death denies Alice too.

Johnny can only watch, mesmerized and incredulous, as Alice gasps, sucking in the mixture of blood and void, drinking it into herself. Her eyelids flutter and open. Veins in her neck bulge and purple, angry lines like lightning down her neck, across her chest, climbing down her arms and legs. When Johnny looks at her face, the hollows of her cheeks have deepened, the whites of her eyes are stained and murky, irises a seafoam stab in glassy black.

"Alice," the word is a whisper of wonder and terror and hope.

Alice sucks in a groan, a monster waking.

"Alice?" Johnny grows frantic, yanking the knife from Alice's spine and dropping it onto the carpet. "Alice, are you okay?"

Alice, unblinking, looks into the gash in the wall, where a thing that once was Lucy wraps shifting tentacles around the opening. Cracks spiral out. Wallpaper tears and drywall crumbles, powdering the surrounding tile.

"What have you done?" Alice asks, voice hoarse and grumbling.

Behind Alice, the void rears up, a hole torn in one world, a spectral snapshot into another. Swirling black, glimmers of distant stars rising like a hunched beast, towering over Alice like a demon—or savior. Before the specter of her terror, Johnny cries out, "Nothing! NOTHING! I just wanted us to be together. I just wanted to make it work!"

"You wanted to change me," Alice says, rising from the couch. Her body lifts, hovering in the air, which cradles her, places her on her feet. "You thought I needed fixing, that I was broken."

Johnny scrambles to her feet. A loud crack comes from the wall, and the sliding glass door shatters. Beyond the patio is endless black, a cosmos freckled by distant stars. The rainbow hue of a kaleidoscope galaxy glows from a place Johnny will never reach.

"You wanted to possess me. Take me away from every other person, every other thing. Have my heart all for yourself." A gust sweeps through the apartment. Plates and cups and silverware rip past from the kitchen. Lucy's crate, the coffee table, then the sofa are sucked into the void. Its vacuum tugs at Johnny's flesh, rippling it and pulling at her clothes, but she remains planted where she is, as if Alice's gravity is stronger than the pull of the emptiness around them.

Johnny always wanted her and Alice to be the only two real things in the universe. But to see it like this, to have it realized, feels lonely, feels wrong. "I just wanted you to love me," Johnny says, as tile falls away beneath her feet. All around them, earth's crust opens and walls crumble down into unknowable depth. In every direction, emptiness, thundering rock, roaring flame, the deep belly growl of the vacancy of infinite space.

Alice rises, a singular thing of void and beast and woman, magnificent and terrible in her beauty. A cascade of popping sounds as her sternum cracks. She tosses her head back, ribs ripping through her flesh one after another in quick time. Black blood spatters Johnny's cheeks, hot then warm then cold in a flash, freezing, frigid enough to burn. Where should be a beating heart sits a shriveled clump of muscle, twitching where it should beat.

"Here I am," Alice says, voice low and hoarse. "Broken. Here is what you want." Her arms extend, palms flipped upward, crucified. "Take it."

Johnny steps to the edge of the remaining floor, a ragged pillar over a whistling unknown. Her toes curl at the ledge for grip and she reaches, bone shards of Alice's desiccated ribcage carving out strips of flesh on either side of Johnny's hand, but she pushes past, until her fingers trace the ruined, heart-shaped thing in Alice's chest. She clenches around the shuddering mass.

"That's it," Alice says.

Johnny pulls.

Muscle squelches in her fist, sinew tearing, tissue giving way. She frees it with a final, nauseating pop. Alice's shoulders jerk forward, her back curling concave, gaze fixing on Johnny as black liquid tunnels up from the dark O of her throat and drips from the corner of her lips.

Johnny cups Alice's heart in both hands, a baby bird, a precious thing plucked from a bony nest. The twist of joining muscle, the frayed arteries limp, tassels from how they tore. Its twitching is erratic. Stillness peppered by violent spasms. When it presses against Johnny's lips, Alice combs Johnny's hair with her fingertips, and Johnny thinks of all she has done for this slimy, thumping thing. All she would still do.

"Go on," Alice says. "It's yours."

The organ slides against Johnny's front teeth, easily punctured by her right incisor. The texture of it is nothing short of divine, the flavor metallic and bitter. Full-bodied. Johnny bites and chews, savoring the complex profile. Her cheeks fill with Alice's gnashed meat. Chewing and rolling it over her tongue, sucking the taste down her throat in greedy pulls. And when the taste of blood has drained, and Alice's heart is a torn, bland mess of fibers in Johnny's mouth, she swallows, gulp by thick gulp.

Johnny looks to her lover. Her horrid and heavenly lover, splayed in front of her, and laughing—still laughing. Singularity in her eyes.

"Is it everything you hoped?" Alice asks as the void presses tendrils through her eye sockets. "Was it worth it?"

Dark goo pours down Alice's cheeks like runny eggs. Johnny screams, a desperate, strangled sound, wrapping arms around her lover's waist.

But Alice is going. Lucy's featherless wings explode from Alice's back, exposed bone framing raw musculature, dripping in viscera. Claws curl at the wing tips. Alice throws her head back, darkness leaking from her eye sockets, streaming down her throat, bubbling through gurgling gasps of forced air. Johnny holds tight as the wings stretch. They beat the air, fanning heat from teasing flames beneath, inciting them to rise. The scent of burnt hair, baking flesh.

Somewhere, a phone buzzes. Johnny hears the tight rattle. She turns to look, finding the flames have died and the vastness of space all around her. Alice's phone floats some thirty feet away, rotating at eye level, unaffected by the void's pull. The screen lights up. It buzzes.

Alice's wings raise the pair of them higher, away from the phone, away from the flames, away from the incoming call. Johnny feels she should answer, but equally strong is the urge to let Alice carry her away, into the dark, into the black hole, past the limits of the event horizon.

Alice twists away from Johnny's grasp, her leathery flesh slipping from Johnny's hold.

The phone buzzes.

Alice is leaving. Writhing upward. Johnny's hold is slipping. She clings to her lover, but what is left of Alice? What is left of Johnny's dream? Nothing. A gaping hole where a heart should be and an inky void where those glacial eyes once met Johnny's. Nothing is left and having devoured her heart, finally holding it in cupped hands, taking it into herself, somehow still felt empty.

With a final thrust of wings, Alice slides from Johnny's grip. Johnny's surprised when she hovers in place, pushed away just slightly with each flip of Alice's wings. She has to get to the phone, she realizes. Alice is beyond her reach, but she cannot be alone, and something else has been calling to her all this time.

Johnny swims through space. Hand over hand, she strokes the vacuum, fighting zero gravity, glancing back as her lover flies farther and farther from her reach. Progress is abysmal, great swathes of effort gaining only inches toward the buzzing phone. Still, she pushes on. The familiar number scrolls across the illuminated screen, 0-112-358-1321. If she could just reach it, if she could just answer, she knows, just knows, there will be some answer on the other end of the line.

Johnny kicks her legs. Reaches, wishing she could dislocate her shoulder from the socket. She kicks again, slicing space with cupped hands, beating against the impossible emptiness. The phone buzzes. She reaches a final time, and this reach puts her fingertips in contact with the screen. Grit presses her forward, pushing the phone securely into her hand.

0-112-358-1321 calling.

She slides to answer.

0-112-358-1321 missed call.

She tries to open the phone, to call back the number.

Password required.

"Fuck!" Johnny screams. All the hope, all the wishes she's stowed away in her heart, all the possible futures she and Alice might have shared fall away. "Fuck you!" Johnny cries, hot tears gathering in her eyes, refusing to slide down her cheeks for lack of gravity. She squeezes the phone, wishing she could crush it in her palm, wishing Alice would've carried her off to whatever vacuous end awaited them. She is truly alone. Surrounded by stars and utter black, she will die alone, with no one to hear her sobs. Hungry, thirsty, with only the cold comfort of oblivion. Miserably alone.

The phone buzzes. **I will not give up on her.**

Incoming call 0-112-358-1321.

Johnny sucks in a breath. Slides to answer. The call time display ticks backward 0:03 to 0:02 to 0:01.

"Hello?"

SATURDAY

Johnny joins me in the in-between place, on a day that feels like Saturday. The in-between is a valley of velvet grasses, flowering purple. Honeybees cruise low near the blossoms, their wings vibrating in a pleasant hum. Beside us, a wide river flows, so clear we can see straight to the sandy bottom. The river is fed by a tumbling waterfall. Rainbow mist shimmers over the froth, and at its base, a herd of wild horses, chestnut, palomino, and bay, gallop through the surrounding wood. We spot them only in flashes, for the trees are thick and tangled and older than memory. Between the steady percussion of hoofbeats, the rushing water, and the hum of honeybees, the in-between is filled with quiet music. It is always spring here. Warm, with a gentle breeze, and we have no natural predators.

This is the place Johnny imagines in the tranquil moments preceding sleep. It is her vision of a perfect world, beauty spilled to its fullest. She glances at the powder blue clouds, the blushing sky, twin moons that smile down from their places above a far off, snow-crested mountain top—then looks at me. We are two halves of a split whole.

I, the Johnny who watches.

She, the Johnny who lives.

"Who are you?" she asks, taking me in like her own reflection, warped through a carnival mirror. "You look like me."

And I say, "I'm the you who remembers."

Slowly, her gaze passes over each of my features, *our* features. "Remembers what?"

She draws closer, craning her head as if to make sure I have a profile, am not just some in-between dream. "All the times we've lived this week before," I say.

With all she's seen, snowfall in summer, tsunamis through city streets, English bulldogs transformed to shape-shifting horrors, she doesn't fight the logic. This time, she doesn't make an argument for physics or souls or the indivisibility of consciousness. Johnny is tired. We are both so tired. "It felt familiar," Johnny says. "Monday, at the café. I thought it was déjà vu."

I tell her, "I was watching at the Speakeasy, when we saw her again."

She asks, "Did you know what would happen?"

My stomach aches with guilt's tender bruise, and **I cannot look at her. Cannot look at myself.**

"Why didn't you stop it?" she asks. "Why didn't you stop me?"

"I tried," I say, the weight of my failures heavy on my chest. "I called. I texted—and the sign…" A breeze bends the flowers at my feet.

It wasn't enough. She doesn't have to say it. The words, unspoken, hang humid between us.

"**This has happened before**." Johnny flushes with a shame that's all too familiar.

"Yes." I explain as best I can, that I was there, I was with her, watching when I could and always remembering and always trying to spare her. Always. I tell her I know about Monday and Tuesday, Wednesday and Thursday and Friday because **I've lived it and watched it, lived it and watched it** so many times each conscious moment is inscribed in my memory, an indelible brand.

"It was you. The calls and texts. Everything else," she says.

We remember the oven clock and the billboard and the shape of tuna.

"You could've stopped it sooner," I say, sliding the guilt toward her, but wondering if there was something, anything else I could've done. "It never works. You never answer, not until Friday."

Johnny's cheeks bulge with her clenching jaw. "**You could've done more**. You should've warned me." She turns, taking a few steps away and leaving flattened grass and crushed petals behind her.

"**You always want to stay**," I call across the distance between us. It's louder than I meant it to be, more accusing.

"How many times?" Johnny asks, eyes toward the double moons, her voice quivering.

The truth is, I lost count a long time ago, but I say something else that's true. "Enough."

"Five?" she asks, then spins on her heel. "Ten? Fifty?"

"Enough."

Johnny stiffens, squaring her shoulders with mine. "You should have done something!" she yells.

"I did!" A flock of parrots flee from the nearest thicket of trees, squawking as they fly. Heat pricks at the corners of my eyes. "You never listen! You never listen to me. All you can see is her. All you care about is Alice, no matter what she does to you. No matter who she turns you into. You don't listen to me, you don't listen to anyone."

"What is happening here?" She chuckles with an aimless rage. "Why is this happening?"

"I don't know," I say.

Johnny slumps down, cradling her knees. Beside her, the river laps lazily onto the pebbled shore. "Do we have to go back?"

For the first time this week, I feel a flicker of hope, the possibility of change, of a new ending. "No," I say, almost too quickly. "**We can** move forward, **leave the past where it is**."

In the field, standing alone against the current of grasses appears a door, formed in the image of the very same one that hangs in Alice's apartment. Red paint flakes around a brass knob, an empty coat hook hanging at the center. "We never have to do it again, if we go through there." The cosmos has a sense of humor. It is the door out, the one Johnny almost uses on Tuesday and Friday, but never walks through. Never.

Johnny looks at the door, rubs her lips against her teeth as if considering. "Will Alice be there?"

"I don't know," I say. "I don't think so."

Johnny nods, gaze drifting away from the door. Our path out. "Does she ever get better?" Johnny doesn't meet my eyes when she asks, "In all the versions you've seen, are we ever happy?"

I come to Johnny's side, placing my hand gently on her shoulder. "No."

Johnny squints and tenses, pushing back a wave of bitter disappointment. "She never changes?"

"I don't think she can," I say. "I don't think she knows how to."

Rays of light permeate the edges of the door, capturing Johnny's attention. "What's out there?"

We both look into the warm glimmer shining at its edges. "I don't know that either," I say. "Something different." The soft glow folds around red paint, turning it pink. "Something else. Something we've never tried before."

A honeybee lands briefly on her shoulder before buzzing up, up, up and away. "Do you want to go through there?" Johnny asks.

"I—"

"Do you want to give up?"

Agonizing pain ricochets through my center. *I don't. I don't. I don't. But we must.* "I do," I say. "We deserve a chance, just a shot at something better. She can't love us, Johnny. You know. I know. We've done everything we can. I know we want it worse than anything. We want a life with Alice so bad **we broke** the universe. But it doesn't want us. It always hurts. I don't think it's meant for us."

Tears drop silently down Johnny's cheeks, carving a trail through dried blood.

"I think we should go through there. **But we** have to agree. If I go through without you, Monday starts all over again."

Johnny hugs herself tighter. She stares at the door for a long time, eyes tracing its shape, up, down, and around, then resting on the knob.

"It's gotta be better, Johnny." It's too close, the promise of something new. It's sticky. I dare to believe it might be real this time, it might be possible that I **can** fix her, **heal** the fissures in Johnny that make her a killer, that return her to Alice in loop after loop, stand in the gaps she thinks Alice can fill. **Imagine** me, imagining Johnny in my arms, moving through that door together, our flesh stitching, **two severed halves joining as one**. Imagine *us*. And we don't return to the Speakeasy Café. And we never feel the press of those crumbling apartment walls or watch Brynne die or waltz one-two-three, we never taste blood and we never again *wonder if*.

Maybe we rest. Maybe we recycle, are reborn into a different life or mingle with the essential, enigmatic thing that runs living and breathing through all. If the Christians are right, maybe we burn. **But** anything would be better than the slow agony of repeating, of watching, of circling the drain, making the same mistakes again and again, riding the vicious loop all the way to the bottom and always always always finding *nothing* when we get there.

Then all **that inflated promise collapses** in just five words. Johnny says, "I want to try again."

I extend my hand, as I've done countless times before. Even with all I know and all I've seen, all we've been forced to bear, inside me is sick, tiny hope. *Maybe this time, it works.* She reaches to take my hand, but before she does, I ask, "Are you sure?"

"**I'm** sure," she says, grasping my palm. "Just one more time."

I pull Johnny up to her feet. We look at the door then look at one another. "It won't change," I say. "You'll have to watch. You'll remember and I'll forget and in a week we'll end up back here, and it'll be me you're trying to convince."

"Just one more time," she says. "One more try."

We've said this before, a hundred or a thousand or **ten thousand times**, but the decision has cemented in the lines of her face. Settles into faint creases formed over an unhappy lifetime. As I walk to the door, I feel the press of her eyes at my back. "It will hurt." Hand on the knob, I say, "Come with me."

Her arms fold. "You always ask, and I always say no."

When the knob turns, I'm swallowed by glimmering gold light. Its warmth is a bittersweet promise, already **broken**. Before it takes me entirely, I hear two words from the in-between, a place I can no longer see.

"I'm sorry."

SUNDAY

Sunday occurs outside of time. It's unfair to call it Sunday, really, for this very reason. But what else is a person to call the space between a-day-that-feels-like-Saturday and Monday-all-over-again? It is a wedge that is difficult to name and difficult to describe. It is the place where the loop resets.

What happens there is a trade, but not an even one. Slowly, Johnny remembers, and slowly, I forget. I pour myself into her, as if gray matter leaks from my left ear into her right, and with it all the knowledge of what's come before, all the...

Loops. It was loops of watching and trying and helping and failing. She will have to watch, feel the desperate flail of trying to stop it sooner. It will be Johnny calling, texting, putting up billboards (and whispering to fish). It will be Johnny struggling to pull *me* out, to save—

Who were we trying to save?

It's Johnny's turn to watch. Her eyes alight with 100,000 flashes, shame and delight, agony and regret and pleasure. The feelings I see, but I can't quite place the why. What does she—

It feels like a slow flow of molten wax. A lightening. An unburdening. What was noise in my head, a cosmic roar, quiets to a vision of Alice.

Oh, Alice!

To touch her. To share her space. To feel her near me.

I would do anything.

I can change.

Make her love me.

She can change.

We can be happy together.

I know it.

MONDAY

When I spot Alice, head thrown back in laughter at the Speakeasy Café, it's with the vaguest sense that **I've been here before**.

The End

WRITE MY EULOGY ON THE GLORYHOLE BATHROOM STALL

A Short Story by Rae Wilde

Brett Mitchell Kent

Write My Eulogy On The Gloryhole Bathroom Stall
By Rae Wilde

I met god in the men's room at the corner of 4th and Broadway. I don't make a habit of using the men's room, but rain was coming in sideways, landing like bee stings onto my ear and neck. Did a quick one-two look. Didn't see the ladies'. So, I ducked inside, just wanted a respite long enough to phone a rideshare.

My first fear—that I'd find a line of dudes, dicks out, piss streaming—was unfounded. The bathroom sat empty. Empty except for the smell. I slapped my palm to my face but couldn't cover it, urea and shit and stagnant water so thick it turned the air viscous. I whipped out my phone, determined to grab a car and get the fuck out of there, but I moved too quick and flung it. Of course I fucking flung it. And it went careening across the yellow tile, little one-inch squares framed by more filth than grout. It slid into the corner stall, and I wiggled my fingers as I caught up to it, as if I might get ahead of the germs I was about to touch, shake 'em off before they clung to me.

The fluorescent bulb overhead flickered: one, two, three. It was eerie, in that horror-movie-gearing-up-to-the-killing-scene sort of way. But I wrote the goosebumps off to the lasting chill of freezing rain, averted my eyes from the abomination in the toilet—mustard yellow soft serve sprinkled with ruptured hemorrhoid—and leaned into that too cramped corner where my phone glowed.

Looking back, it must've been god that dropped the deuce in there. Face turned away from the thing responsible for one third of the smell, I was eye to eye with the wall. And if not for that, I wouldn't have found it.

A hole.

It was about the size of a fist. Inside was that black-black, that absence of light black, where you can't tell how far it goes. Could've been Mariana's fucking trench in there. I don't know what it was, a calling maybe, but something made me reach. While my left hand secured my phone in my jeans pocket, my right slipped into the hole, careful not to touch the sides. I felt for a stud, insulation, something, but I was halfway to my elbow and when a pinch on my hand made me yank it back. A bug, a spider, a snake, maybe? Three red divots in my knuckles and a pulsing feeling. I'd been bit, and I would've gotten the hell out of there, I would've, if not for what followed.

What began as a twinge of pain rolled to my elbow then armpit. It wrapped around my neck and spread through my core. I didn't realize I'd landed on my ass until my hands braced me from sprawling; but even as I felt mystery grime flake beneath my fingernails, I didn't care.

To call it a *high* would be to trivialize it.

There are seven wonders of the world, people say, and I became the eighth. For the first time, the creator of the universe looked right at me, looked right at me *approvingly*. The rain outside became the constant heartbeat of the world, the fear of germs faded with the recognition that no lifeform was truly apart from myself.

Time slipped; the separation between the atoms of my flesh and air around me dissipated. My body and spirit swelled with peace and warmth, enveloping and smothering every painful thing. It was a state of being so close to how I'd heard religious folk imagine heaven, and yet so much more and outside of understanding that the descriptor falls short. And I sat alone beside the gloryhole bathroom stall, alone with god, and it was certainly good.

My phone was dead and the rain had stopped when reality returned. If anyone came in, I didn't notice. Meeting god must've stretched me somewhere inside, because while I didn't have the dull ache in my head of a hangover, I had the prickling anxiety of a new space opened up beneath my rib cage, a birth of absence, and the vacancy there itched deeper than skin and nerve.

I didn't catch a ride share. I walked the three miles home.

Night air was cool and crisp. The storm had dumped all the humidity from the air into the streets. My breaths were easy but shallow. Each step drew me further from 4th and Broadway. I stopped several times. Considered going back. But I figured Alyssa would be worried, a notion confirmed when I slipped through our apartment door to find her pacing and frantic.

"Where the *fuck* have you been? I've been calling."

I held up my phone screen, rapid pressing the buttons to no effect.

"Shit, I was worried."

"Sorry, I—"

"What happened to your hand?"

I glanced down to find the bite marks had turned from red pricks to angry, purple vines clutched around my palm. "Bug bite, or something. I think." My voice sounded distant, and Alyssa pressed.

I tried to explain god.

"You must've gotten stuck by a needle. Lucky as shit you didn't overdose. Actually, Sam, we should get you checked out, just in case." She moved to where her coat hung on the wall.

"No, no." I dropped my purse on the counter. "I'm fine, just need some sleep."

She argued for five minutes more before surrendering to the bathroom to brush her teeth. I rehearsed lines over and over in my head, but couldn't come up with a way to get her to go back with me, not tonight. The empty space beneath my ribs hummed as I settled into bed. I had to go back. To be with god. To feel unburdened and wholly seen. But I told myself it could wait until tomorrow, when Alyssa was rested and her curiosity might get the best of her.

Uneasily, we slept.

In the men's room at 4th and Broadway, Alyssa clutched her hand over her nose, just like I had.

"Christ, Sam."

"Just look."

I tugged her by her shirt sleeve, candy pink against the jittery fluorescent glow of dying bulbs and grime-yellow tile. She squinted to read the graffiti surrounding the hole.

"*Margret Ashbury is a whore. Dylan: Fridays 6-7pm, suck & fuck.* Very nice, Sam."

A flash of impatience made me bite back a retort, but my eye caught the words scribbled in red sharpie beneath the gloryhole. *The devil made me cum.*

"I see it, okay? Your hand looks…"

Purple tendrils shot from an indigo center, swelling that pulsed offbeat from my pumping blood.

"We need to get you to a doctor. What if a black widow was hiding in there? You could have sepsis or something."

"Please, just try it. I can't explain it. There's no way you can understand unless you——"

"Hep C. HIV. Sam, no fucking chance I'm putting my hand in there. I humored you, alright? I came, I smelled, I saw it. Let's fucking go."

The vacant space inside my ribs expanded like heated air, a void that screamed without sound. I wanted to reach behind the wall, to grasp for more, but I let Alyssa walk me out, even agreed to lunch and half-listened when she brought up that coworker who steals snacks from the communal fridge again. Better if she didn't realize, I figured. Would make it easier to sneak back.

The thirty-five-minute lunch stretched on, an infinite purgatory of watching my lover butter bread, draw soup to her lips spoonful by too-small spoonful, sip sprite, ice cubes clinking against her teeth.

"I'm not hungry, really," I told Alyssa, I told the waitress.

I offered my card before the waitress brought the bill, and as I signed the check, the lie came out like a song. "Totally forgot, promised to head into work for a few."

Suspicion crinkled her freckled nose. "Thought you were off today."

"I am." I got up. "New hire, helping to get him oriented. Rob, lives with his mom type, not gonna last."

Alyssa shrugged and her expression relaxed. I leaned across the table for a parting kiss, half wondering how I conjured Rob so quickly, half walking the route back to 4th and Broadway in my mind.

The walk was an impatient blur. When my fingers met the metal door handle, the aching void in my sternum nearly ripped my breastbone in half. I rolled my sleeve to the elbow, coy flicks of my wrist, cherishing the moments before my fist disappeared into the dark. Seconds ticked by like sludge as I waited, eager for the little prick and the ecstasy that followed.

Then, the slice made me cry out. I yanked my arm back out of instinct, but bliss gobbled me up before I had time to observe the injury. And it didn't matter anymore. I floated. Everything was fine. God spoke.

Does it hurt? He asked. *You're doing so well. Does it hurt?*

"Yes," I mumbled.

A slump brought me flat down, my sandal sliding off my foot.

I want more, god said.

"Of me?" The words rolled over my lolling tongue.

Give me more of you.

I dragged myself across the tile, inch by impossible inch, eyes rolling and vision blurred. My head grew too heavy, flopped to one side. I tossed a crooked arm toward the hole, and almost thought I saw empty space where the tip of my pinky usually was.

I probably saw it.

But it didn't matter.

My aim floundered, hand missing the hole entirely, but my elbow made it into the black, and no sooner had I offered it did god accept it, hot agony racing up my nerves, fingertip to armpit.

The most delicious emptiness chased all thoughts and pain away. Only a throbbing remained. It traveled through my blood. It gathered in my center. It congealed between my thighs. God wanted me, intimately, vulnerably. And I wanted to offer myself. In the flickering fluorescent light, I removed my top, let it fall, and when the hem dipped into the toilet, my fingers raced to my pussy instead of saving it. I pressed my left breast against the hole, working myself into a frenzy. I thought of god's teeth. I thought of razored bicuspids, sharpened as only a deity's might be, piercing my areola, shredding the membranes beneath.

I moaned.

The slickness of my pussy lips let my hand slip inside, slowed only by the constraints of my jeans.

"Come on," I said, breathy, impatient, arching my back to press my breast further into the hole. The pressure built with the anticipation, wetness bleeding through my jeans as I kept the rhythm, anxiously awaiting the slice.

Is this a gift?

"Yes," came out like a plea.

I'd already started coming when god freed my nipple from the bounds of my flesh.

There was everything, then: The stinging, the soul-wracking climax, the gentle oblivion.

I collapsed onto the tile. Life-warmth poured down my stomach, my jeans were stained burgundy, and I checked my hand to find my little finger missing and gore flowing from elbow to wrist.

But it didn't matter.

I took a deep breath.

I laid flat.

I studied the water stains on the ceiling.

I let my fingers trace the graffiti.

I hooked my nail into a hardened piece of gum affixed to the toilet paper dispenser.

"Can I stay like this forever?" My voice sounded dreamy, and god didn't answer. I let myself be held by something which had called to me. Maybe all my life it had called to me. And I knew that nothing had ever felt right until this.

I didn't go back to Alyssa's.

My remaining days were hazy. Alyssa kept calling, my parents kept calling, my boss kept calling. Alyssa texted. She said lots of things. Things about losing. Losing her. She named a lot of other things, which didn't matter.

There was knocking sometimes, and I got good at being quiet. Very quiet, until it stopped.

Then nobody was calling. Or texting. Or knocking. And that was good.

The first time god fucked me, he wasn't gentle. It wasn't a romance in any way I'd seen or experienced, but the seduction burned hot and fast and desperate. I'd pulled my jeans and panties down and pressed my pussy right up against the hole like a dog. I wanted to feel god's tongue. I wanted it to plunge inside me, to rip out my cervix with its barbed tip, to gush come and blood until the writing on the bathroom stall was washed away with my liquid, depraved pleasure.

God took my other nipple, my left thumb, my right hand to the wrist.

God had a fat cock and a warm pussy.

I fucked and I got fucked, I gave and I got and I gave pieces away. The pain was gone, even as the blood soaked through my tattered clothing, dried and crusted and flaked off every part of me. I came so hard I pissed myself. Even when hunger had me so weak I passed out, it didn't matter. God was all I needed, god's gifts were abundant and if there was still a world outside that heavy metal door, it didn't need me anymore. And I didn't need it. I'd given Alyssa a chance. I'd tried to show her. Yes, it wasn't my fault she couldn't see. And now she'd never know. She'd never know *him*. She'd never know the fullness of being empty.

Fuck Alyssa.

I squatted in front of god's hole and gave him my ass.

I knew the freedom of giving myself selflessly, of receiving gratefully, of lightening as I was unburdened of my intestines. They made the sound of slop as they went coiling onto the yellow tile. God slurped them up like spaghetti. One long pull and they raced into the gloryhole like a speedy toy train, leaving a slick trail behind like smudged tracks. I'd never been so savored, my body like a sweet wine, ripe for consumption.

I dipped my fingers in dark liquid. On the bathroom door I scribbled, *Resplendent suffering.*

We had braided, god and pain and the cosmos and completion and never-having-been, and my throbbing clitoris. And my flesh could not be parsed from the most intimate particles of the universe. No separation stood between me and the oldest suffering and the first pleasure. God fucked me into nothingness. I consumed carnality in its purest form as god drew my head to the glory hole and beyond it, took me into her pussy as his cock penetrated my throat. Clenching and thrusting and a kind, contented knowing.

God came.

And I blinked from being. A snap in which I relived my many years of existence and my very few days of living. I came to this one reflection:

If I'd known that first rainy day what I know now. If I'd realized what would happen, how Alyssa would spend her birthday crying, how dad would never again hear a phone ring without a stitch of anxiety, that my body would rot on the yellow tiled floor for six days before anyone found me, that the insects would've chewed through my sclera, that shit leaked from my gaping anus at the end, and the mortician felt embarrassed for me and had to tell his wife about it just to throw off some of the shame, my shame. If I'd have known on that first rainy day, I would've shoved my hand into that hole even faster. I would've never taken it out.

ACKNOWLEDGEMENTS

A heartfelt and humble thank you…

To my incredibly supportive family: A book is a labor of love, not only for the author but for everyone around them. You have loved me through the ups and downs (both writing-related and not) and have created space (both literal and metaphorical) for me to work on this fickle craft. None of this could happen without you. I know I talk too much about my stories. Thanks for listening. Thanks for loving me.

To my writing mentor and BFF, C.S. Humble: You have spent countless hours helping me improve. You have recommended reading. You have broken down what works and why. You are still the better writer, but I'm coming for you.

To Tanya, Rachel, Jess, Amanda, Evelyn, Alexis, Sofia, Sapphire, and the many, many other friends I've made in the writing community: Thank you for celebrating with me, laughing with me, being there for the tough moments. What a joy it is to find friends who share this passion.

To Christoph and Leza: Thank you so much for taking a chance on me and my work. I'm so proud to be among your incredible slate of authors.

To the reader: Thank you for trusting me with your time.

ABOUT THE AUTHOR

Rae Wilde (she/her) is a queer woman and author of dark fiction who has also published under the name Rae Knowles. Her work includes *The Stradivarius*, *Merciless Waters*, and *I Do Not Apologize for My Position on Men*. Rae is the author of numerous shorter works, published in magazines and anthologies such as *Dark Matter Ink*, *Nightmare*, and *Ghoulish Tales*. Rae is represented by Carleen Giesler at Arthouse Literary.

ALSO BY CLASH BOOKS

8114
Joshua Hull

THE BODY HARVEST
Michael J. Seidlinger

**THE PINK AGAVE MOTEL
& OTHER STORIES**
V. Castro

HER NEW EYES
T.J. Martinson

THE BLACK TREE ATOP THE HILL
Karla Yvette

THE LONGEST SUMMER
Alexandrine Ogundimu

CATHERINE THE GHOST
Kathe Koja

BELOW THE GRAND HOTEL
Cat Scully